MW00935410

Lost Without You

CYNTHIA BEALS

WESTBOW
PRESS®
A DIVISION OF THOMAS NELSON
& ZONDERVAN

Copyright © 2020 Cynthia Beals.

All rights reserved. No part of this book may be used or reproduced by any means, graphic, electronic, or mechanical, including photocopying, recording, taping or by any information storage retrieval system without the written permission of the author except in the case of brief quotations embodied in critical articles and reviews.

WestBow Press books may be ordered through booksellers or by contacting:

WestBow Press
A Division of Thomas Nelson & Zondervan
1663 Liberty Drive
Bloomington, IN 47403
www.westbowpress.com
1 (866) 928-1240

Because of the dynamic nature of the Internet, any web addresses or links contained in this book may have changed since publication and may no longer be valid. The views expressed in this work are solely those of the author and do not necessarily reflect the views of the publisher, and the publisher hereby disclaims any responsibility for them.

Any people depicted in stock imagery provided by Getty Images are models, and such images are being used for illustrative purposes only. Certain stock imagery © Getty Images.

Scripture quotations are from the ESV® Bible (The Holy Bible, English Standard Version®), copyright © 2001 by Crossway, a publishing ministry of Good News Publishers. Used by permission. All rights reserved.

ISBN: 978-1-9736-8663-7 (sc)
ISBN: 978-1-9736-8664-4 (hc)
ISBN: 978-1-9736-8662-0 (e)

Library of Congress Control Number: 2020903095

Print information available on the last page.

WestBow Press rev. date: 02/17/2020

To my loving husband, Robert, whose support and encouragement helped make this book possible.

Contents

Chapter 1 1
Chapter 2 5
Chapter 3 11
Chapter 4 19
Chapter 5 29
Chapter 6 37
Chapter 7 43
Chapter 8 51
Chapter 9 59
Chapter 10 69
Chapter 11 75
Chapter 12 79
Chapter 13 85
Chapter 14 91
Chapter 15 97
Chapter 16 105
Chapter 17 111
Chapter 18 119
Chapter 19 125
Chapter 20 133
Chapter 21 141
Chapter 22 147
Chapter 23 155
Chapter 24 161
Chapter 25 169
Chapter 26 179
Chapter 27 183
Chapter 28 189
Chapter 29 193
Chapter 30 197
Chapter 31 207
Epilogue 219

Chapter 1

Nicole let the Jeep Wrangler roll to a stop at the curb. Turning off the engine, she leaned over the steering wheel and stared up at the modest Cape Cod in front of her. A frown furrowed her forehead as she studied the house on the small bank of grass. She remembered a lawn that had been the envy of the neighborhood. Now it looked barren, with brown patches and dandelions overtaking it. The house itself was in bad need of a fresh coat of paint.

The Brennans, she remembered, had taken great pride in their home, especially the yard. Lee had kept it immaculate. Nicole remembered the beautiful annuals Deborah had planted every spring that lined the sidewalk up to the front stoop. Beautiful zinnias and petunias used to usher people up the walk to the mahogany front door. Nicole could not remember ever seeing any dandelions in the front yard.

And the house—Nicole barely recognized it. Oh, it was the same Cape Cod-style house with country-blue siding and white trim and shutters, but where it used to shine and gleam, now it looked aged and neglected.

What on earth? she wondered. The Lee and Deborah she had known would never have allowed this to happen. Nicole chewed her bottom lip as she sat back in her seat. *Maybe they don't even live here anymore,* she mused. That made more sense than what she saw in front of her. Maybe she had made a mistake in coming.

A still voice inside of her assured her gently that she had made the right choice, no matter how it turned out. Besides, there was no turning back now. Nicole let out a soft sigh and bowed her head. "Okay, Lord," she whispered. "If this is what You want me to do, You'll have to give me the words because I sure don't have them."

Taking another deep breath, Nicole grabbed her purse from the passenger seat, opened her door, and stepped out into the road. She noticed the other homes up and down the quiet street. Unlike Deborah's, they all seemed well kept up. Shaking her head, Nicole made her way up the steps set in the small front bank and down the short walk to the covered front stoop.

Nicole pressed the small button next to the weathered mahogany door and listened intently for the sound of footsteps, but all she heard was silence. Hesitating a moment, Nicole raised her hand and rapped on the door. Wondering if maybe Deborah was not home, Nicole debated whether she should leave and come back later. Maybe Deborah was out of town. Nicole's thoughts clashed against each other. It had taken three hundred miles of driving to calm her nerves. She was not giving up now. Nicole pushed her short, wavy hair behind her left ear, hesitating as she looked back down to the street, where her car was parked.

Maybe I should go get something to eat and try again later, she thought. Deciding that would work, she turned to walk back down the walkway. Just as she started down the walk, Nicole heard the door open behind her.

"Yes?" a voice said.

Nicole turned back around and stopped short. The lady who stood in front of her did not in any way resemble the Deborah she remembered. This lady wore no makeup, and her hair … that was the biggest surprise. The Deborah she had known had been a redhead.

This stranger in front of her was nearly gray. And not the soft, warm gray like she remembered her grandma having, but a faded, wiry gray.

"Can I help you?" the lady in front of her asked again, this time a little bit more annoyed.

That was Deborah's voice, no doubt about it. Nicole swallowed the lump in her throat and took a step toward her.

"Hi, Deborah," she said. "It's me, Nicole."

Nicole watched as Deborah's gray-blue eyes went from confusion to dawning to contempt. The searing look Deborah gave her made Nicole take a step back. She suppressed the urge to turn and run as she met the older woman's gaze. She deserved everything that Deborah wanted to give her. Anger, contempt, insults—all of it. But after it was all said and done, Nicole hoped Deborah would be able to give her what she had come for—forgiveness.

Deborah could only stare. This couldn't be real. *Lord, why? After all that I've been through? Haven't I suffered enough? No, this is too much! I don't have to deal with her too.* Straightening her shoulders, Deborah bored her eyes into Nicole, who didn't back down. She almost hadn't recognized her. It had been five years since she had last seen her. Good riddance, too, as far as she was concerned, after what she had done to Marc—to her family. Deborah took a deep breath as the pain pierced through her heart. It was a pain that she had lived with for too long.

"What do you want?" she demanded.

"I …" Nicole stumbled over her words, clearly uncomfortable. "I would like to talk with you if I could, Deborah. Please."

Deborah leaned her hand on the doorjamb, blocking Nicole's entrance. "You've got a lot of nerve. There's nothing you have to say that I want to hear."

Nicole took the force of her words without flinching. Her eyes watered as she focused them back on Deborah. "I am so sorry for what I did, Deborah, to Marc and to you. I know it was terrible, and

I have no excuse, but I've changed. I'm not that same person." Nicole paused and took a shaky breath. "I know I don't deserve it, Deborah, but I've come to ask for your forgiveness."

Nicole took another deep breath before Deborah could speak and continued, "I ... I've written Marc and asked for his forgiveness, but I haven't heard back from him. I just hope in time he can forgive me, but I needed to come here and ask for your forgiveness too."

Deborah was speechless as she listened to Nicole stammer on. Was she serious? Deborah felt a deep burning rise up inside of her, unleashing its full fury until she could no longer contain it.

Coldly, she spat, "You'll never get Marc's forgiveness. It's too late for that. Marc was killed in action six months ago."

Nicole looked as though she had been sucker punched. She took a step back from the words Deborah had hurled at her. Deborah felt a sense of pleasure at the pain she saw in Nicole's eyes.

"A part of Marc died the day you left," Deborah continued, "and I will never forgive you for that! Not as long as I live!"

Deborah stepped back into the house and slammed the door shut in Nicole's ashen face. As she leaned her back against the door, the tears came unabated. Deborah slid down the door to the cold, tiled floor. She put her head in her hands as her body rocked with renewed anguish.

Nicole staggered back, the full force of Deborah's words washing over her, turning her stomach to stone. She turned and walked blindly down the walk and then down the steps. Opening her car door, she slid behind the wheel and sat there.

Marc was dead? It couldn't be true. A realization from deep inside pushed its way outward, her body shaking with the truth. Deborah wouldn't lie about this. No mother would ever lie about something like that. Not even to get back at her. Numb, Nicole turned the key in the ignition and pulled away from the curb.

Chapter 2

Nicole lay on top of a faded comforter staring up at the popcorn ceiling tile that was yellowed and stained. She couldn't remember how long she had driven or how she had ended up here. It could have been twenty minutes, or it could have been two hours. All she remembered was that after driving aimlessly around for a while, she had suddenly become so tired that she pulled into the first motel she found.

As soon as she had checked in, she pulled around to her room, let herself in, and curled up into a ball on the double bed in the middle of the run-down room. It was only after she gave in to the tears that she finally fell into an exhausted sleep. Three hours later when she woke up she did not feel rested. Instead, remorse and guilt washed over her anew. She couldn't breathe, couldn't think.

"Is this what You sent me here for, Lord?" she asked through fresh tears. "Was it to punish me?"

Nicole waited for a response, but all she heard was the sound of traffic whizzing by on the interstate that ran next to the hotel. Her cell phone buzzed on the nightstand next to the bed. Nicole forced herself to sit up as she reached across the bed to pick it up.

Four missed calls.

Nicole looked at the caller ID as she grabbed a fistful of Kleenexes from the night stand. The same number had called repeatedly. Rubbing the wadded-up Kleenex across her sore nose, Nicole punched in the number on her phone.

"Nicole, are you okay?" the voice on the other end practically screeched in her ear. "I've been trying to get hold of you for hours! I've been so worried!"

Nicole glanced over at the alarm clock by the bed. It was almost seven. How had time slipped away like that? Fresh guilt poured over her as she raised her balled-up hand to her forehead and leaned forward.

"I'm so sorry, Kathee. I got to the motel here and just collapsed. I never turned my phone back up."

There was a slight pause at Kathee's end before she spoke, her voice softer. "I gather it didn't go well with Deborah?"

A raspy chuckle escaped out of Nicole's throat before she could stop it.

"Are you okay?" her friend asked.

Nicole rubbed her eyes with her free hand. Kathee Jewel was her best friend. They had met four years earlier, during a time when Nicole was at a low point in her life. It had been Kathee's deep-rooted faith and friendship that were responsible for Nicole turning her life around and finding her own faith. When Nicole had accepted Christ, Kathee had been right there next to her. They had been like sisters ever since.

Kathee had listened to Nicole when she told her of her desire to make things right with Marc. She had supported her decision and agreed that it was the right thing to do. When there had been no response back from Marc, Kathee had supported Nicole's decision to seek Deborah. The timing had seemed right. She had just finished nursing school and hadn't started looking for a job yet. Nicole thought it would be a good time to go see Deborah before she started her new life. Now it felt like a big mistake on so many levels.

Taking a deep breath, Nicole said, "No, I'm not. Not really."

"I'm sorry, Nicole. What happened?"

Nicole shut her eyes and leaned back against the headboard. "Kathee … Marc is dead."

Nicole heard Kathee's quick intake of breath. "What? Oh, no, Nicole! When? How?"

"Deborah said he died six months ago in Afghanistan. She really didn't give me any details. At least, I don't think she did. My mind shut down when she said the words."

"I am so sorry, Nicole. How awful!"

"Guess that's why I never heard back from him." Nicole wiped tears away with the back of her hand. "I don't know if he even received my letter. Kathee, what if he died not knowing …" Sobs interrupted her, taking the air out of her breath before she could finish the thought that had plagued her since she had left Deborah's. It was too much for her to contemplate.

"Nicole, listen to me. You can't beat yourself up like this. You don't know that Marc didn't receive your letter. He just may not have had a chance to write back. You gave him news that he never expected to hear. He probably needed time to let it soak in."

"Well, I'll never know. Not now. How am I supposed to live with that? I don't even know why I came. Deborah is never going to be able to forgive me, and I don't blame her. I'll never be able to forgive myself." Nicole put her head in the palm of her free hand, sobbing uncontrollably.

"Nicole, you've already received forgiveness. Remember?" Kathee gently reminded her. "Do you remember the peace you felt when you received Christ's love and forgiveness?"

"Yes," Nicole said as she wiped her nose with the back of her sleeve.

Nicole remembered the night four years ago when Kathee had led her to the Lord after a Bible study. She remembered the peace she had felt when she had confessed her sins and surrendered herself to the Lord. She had never felt such joy and contentment before that. But most of all, it had been the peace she had felt knowing her sins had been forgiven.

But now …

"I think I should just come home, Kathee. There's nothing here for me now. Deborah is never going to be able to forgive me."

"Listen to me, Nicole," Kathee said quietly. "You have to remember that God has His hand in this. We may not understand why, but He does have a reason."

"What do you mean?"

"I mean maybe this is more about grace than it is about forgiveness. Maybe you were sent there to help Deborah heal."

"Oh, I don't see how. You didn't see her, Kathee. She had nothing but pure hate in her eyes when she looked at me."

"You told me that she's a Christian, right?"

"Right, but Kathee, she's changed. I barely recognized that person I saw today."

"Well, so have you. I think you should go see her one more time. You drove all that way; what do you have to lose?"

"Definitely not my pride; I left that at her front door this morning." Nicole raked her fingers through her short, blond hair as she chewed on Kathee's words. "Okay, I'll go see Deborah again in the morning."

"Good. You know I'll be praying for you."

"Yeah, I know," Nicole said with a soft smile. "You're a good friend, Kathee."

"Right back at ya, girlfriend."

Nicole sat up straight as she tugged a fresh Kleenex out of the box next to her on the rumpled bed.

"Different subject," she said. "How are the kids? Is everyone getting along?"

Kathee chuckled as she answered. "They're doing great! They played so hard this afternoon with their new Slip 'n Slide, which, thank you very much for that. You really didn't have to."

"I was glad to. It's the least I could do after all you've done for me. I'm just happy that they're enjoying it. How about Abby? Did she like it too?"

"You should have seen her, Nicole! She had a blast! I took lots of pictures of the four of them. Anyhow, it tuckered them all out. They crashed after dinner while watching *Aladdin*."

"Oh." Disappointment seeped through Nicole's voice. "I was hoping to catch Abby before she went to sleep."

"I'm sorry, Nicole. Do you want me to see if she's awake, maybe?"

"No, don't disturb her. Besides, there's no waking her up once she's out. Just give her a big hug and tell her that her mommy loves her and misses her."

"Will do," Kathee assured, her voice softening. "You know you don't have to worry. She's no problem, and the boys absolutely adore her."

Nicole pictured Kathee's three boys. Josiah was the oldest at eight, Jonathan was six, and Jacob, her youngest, had just turned five and was closest in age to Abby, her daughter, who had turned four last November. The boys had always been kind and protective of Abby from the first time they met. Nicole knew her daughter was being well taken care of and loved.

"I know, Kathee. I appreciate what you're doing so much. You have no idea."

"Hey, that's what friends are for. Now, don't fret about Abby. I plan on spoiling her rotten."

A chuckle escaped Nicole's lips. "Great. There'll be no living with her when I get back."

After saying goodbye, Nicole hit the *end* button on her phone and let out a wisp of a sigh. Tomorrow was not going to be fun, no matter how she looked at it.

Chapter 3

Deborah shuffled into her kitchen. The blinds were drawn down against the early morning light, leaving the kitchen dark. Elijah, her golden retriever, nudged Deborah's leg as she opened the pantry door.

"Hang on, Elijah. Your food is coming." Bending over, Deborah reached into the large bag of Purina Dog Chow, scooped out a large amount, and filled the ceramic dog dish next to the back slider. "There you go."

Elijah responded by going to the bowl and gobbling the food down. Deborah shook her head as she headed through the formal dining room into the front hall. Sleep had been elusive last night. She had tossed and turned, unable to get comfortable or to shake Nicole's visit. When she finally did manage to fall asleep, she was plagued with dreams that she did not remember when she woke up. She just remembered feeling a terrible, deep sense of loss.

Reaching the front door, Deborah opened it. She sighed as she saw that the paperboy had once again missed the front porch and thrown the paper next to the sidewalk. Pulling her bathrobe tighter around her, she stepped down the stairs and bent over to retrieve the *Daily News*. She didn't know why she still got the paper. There was never anything in it she wanted to read. Lee was the one who had liked to sit and read the paper every morning with his coffee. A deep heaviness settled on her at the thought of her husband.

Picking up the paper, Deborah turned to go back up the steps. As she reached the top step, she felt a pain rip through her head. It only worsened as she made her way to the door, making her feel disoriented. She grabbed hold of the doorjamb, trying to stay on her feet. Fear gripped her as she tried to focus on getting inside. She needed to get to the phone in the living room. Something wasn't right. Taking a few uncertain steps, she made it only as far as the middle of the hall before she collapsed with a heavy *thud* on the floor.

The sky had clouded up as Nicole drove from her motel to Deborah's house. After she had hung up with Kathee, Nicole had prayed and then opened her Bible. She had found herself drawn to the book of Ruth. Nicole had always been touched by Ruth's devotion to her mother-in-law and her refusal to leave Naomi's side.

As she pulled up once more to Deborah's house, Nicole threw up a prayer. "I'm not Ruth, Lord, but if You want me to be here, then I'm here. I'll leave the details to You."

Throwing her car door open, Nicole stepped out and walked once more up to the front door. She was halfway there when she noticed the front door ajar. Alarm filled her, and she hesitated for a brief second before hurrying to the door..

"Deborah!" she called as she rushed in and found the older woman lying in the hallway. Elijah sat at her head, whimpering quietly. Dropping her purse on the tiled entranceway floor, Nicole rushed to Deborah's side.

"Shhhh," she whispered as she patted the golden retriever's head. Kneeling, she took Deborah's wrist in her hand and felt for a pulse. She let out a soft breath of relief when she found a faint one.

"What happened, boy?"

Elijah answered with another whimper as he lay down at Deborah's head, refusing to leave his mistress's side.

"It's okay, boy. I'm going to get her some help."

Nicole went back to where she had dropped her purse. Opening it, she reached in and pulled her cell out. She punched in 911 as she made her way back to kneel next to Deborah.

"Nine-one-one, what is your emergency?"

"It's my mother-in-law. I found her unconscious in her home."

Nicole gave the 911 operator the address and hit *end* on the phone with a reassurance that help was on the way. Leaning over Deborah, Nicole gently pushed her hair back out of her eyes.

"It's going to be okay, Deborah. Help's on the way. Hang in there, okay?"

Deborah let out a small moan. "Lee ..."

Nicole paused. She had no idea where Marc's dad was or how to get hold of him. Leaning down, Nicole whispered in her ear. "You're going to be okay, Deborah. Do you hear me? Hang in there."

Nicole sat in the waiting room outside the intensive care unit. An hour ago, a code blue had been called. Nicole knew what that meant. Someone's heart had stopped. She had watched helplessly as nurses, doctors, respiratory techs, and every other available personnel rushed by her open door and entered the ICU. Nicole knew that Deborah was not the only patient in there, but in the pit of her stomach, she knew. Deborah was in big trouble.

Walking back to the chair where she had been holding her lonely vigil, Nicole sat perched on the edge. Silently, she sent up another prayer for the Lord to intervene and help all the doctors and nurses as they worked to save Deborah's life. It had been three hours since Deborah had been brought in by ambulance. Nicole had followed in her own car. She had told everyone from the EMS attendants to the nurse at the front desk that she was Deborah's daughter-in-law.

Not a total lie, Nicole rationalized. She knew that they wouldn't give her any access to what was going on with Deborah if they thought she wasn't family.

Nervously, she got up and walked to the doorway for the umpteenth time. She knew that she could pick up the phone that would connect her immediately to the nurses' station in the ICU and get an answer about what was going on, but she also knew how chaotic things got during a code. No, it was better to let them do their job and wait until things settled down.

Nicole turned back into the room and once more took in her surroundings. Compared to other waiting rooms she had seen, it was about the same. A small counter took up one wall with enough room on it for a small sink, a microwave, and a coffeepot that never seemed to run low. In front of that sat a small, round oak table with four chairs where family members could gather to eat or talk to help pass the time. Nestled on the other side of the room were a recliner, small sofa, and a couple of chairs. All had the same blue-green patterns in them. The walls had the same muted colors, with splashes of pictures in tasteful watercolors.

Mounted up in the far corner was a flat-screen television. The background noise from the local news station filled the emptiness of the room, but Nicole hadn't heard a word of what was being said. They could have said that Martians had landed or that California had finally broken off and fallen into the ocean for all she knew or cared.

Nicole turned her attention back to the doorway when she heard someone enter the waiting room. The doctor who had been attending to Deborah since she had come into ER walked in, his appearance haggard and mussed. He waved Nicole to a nearby chair and took a seat in the chair across from her. Weariness and concern etched his face, his eyes dark with a seriousness that clenched Nicole's stomach. Fear gripped her as she took a deep breath in and waited for the doctor to speak.

"Deborah has had a series of strokes," the doctor began, "that, from what we can tell, have affected her left side and her speech."

"There was a code ..." Nicole began.

"Yes." The doctor nodded as he raked his fingers through dark hair streaked with gray along the fringes. He looked up, met her gaze, and said, "Deborah suffered a heart attack, and her heart stopped."

Nicole sucked in a breath as tears burst through and fell unheeded down her cheeks. "Is she okay?"

The doctor nodded his head in response. "We were able to revive her, but at this point, we don't know how much damage has been done. We're doing more tests now."

Nicole sat silently, absorbing the news the doctor had just given her. Deborah had suffered a stroke and a heart attack. Nicole knew that wasn't good.

"Does Deborah have any other family?" Dr. Theil's question brought her back.

"I'm sorry—I don't remember your name," Nicole said, weariness overtaking her.

"I'm sorry. Dr. Liam Theil."

"Deborah has a husband, Lee, and a son, Tyler. I don't know where Lee is—he wasn't home when I found her. He may be fishing; he loves to fish." Nicole took a breath. She knew she was rambling and took a second to compose herself before continuing. "Marc, her youngest son, was my husband. He died six months ago in Afghanistan."

"I'm sorry for your loss," the doctor said, leaning toward her.

Nicole just shrugged.

Dr. Theil looked in the chart that he held in his hands. "According to her records, Deborah's husband died in a car accident a year ago."

Nicole let the news settle, too shocked to respond. *Poor Deborah* was all she could think. Slowly, she turned her attention back to the doctor. "Marc and I were actually separated when he died. This is the first time I've seen Deborah in five years. I didn't know about Lee."

"What about her other son?" the doctor asked.

"Last I heard, Tyler was living out west. Colorado, I believe." Nicole looked up into the doctor's questioning eyes and shrugged. "Why?"

"It's just that some decisions need to be made regarding Deborah's care."

Understanding dawned on Nicole. "How bad is it? Is she going to recover?"

"Like I said, we don't know the full nature of Deborah's stroke yet. The heart attack she suffered only compounded the situation." The doctor paused and took in a deep breath. "If Deborah is unable to make a decision on her own, a decision may have to be made for her. Right now, as it stands, Deborah will need long-term rehabilitation and care."

"You're talking about a nursing home, aren't you?"

"Under the circumstances—yes. She wouldn't be able to go back home and take care of herself."

Nicole nodded as her mind raced. She tried to envision Deborah in a nursing home all alone and found the idea inconceivable. Deborah would die if she was sent there. Nicole was certain of that.

Looking back at the doctor, Nicole said, "Deborah does not have to go to a nursing home. I can take care of her."

Dr. Theil leaned back, surprised. "Mrs. Brennan, you don't understand what all is entailed. She's going to need twenty-four-hour care. It's very commendable of you to offer to do this, but I don't think you realize what all is involved."

"Yes, I do," Nicole asserted with a nod of her head. "I worked in a nursing home for four years and a VA hospital before that. I got my CRNA, and I just got my nursing degree. I know what is ahead of me. Most of the patients I worked with in the nursing home were stroke patients. Deborah does not need to go to a nursing home. I can take care of her in her own home."

Dr. Theil sighed as he sat back in his chair. "We'll see what we can do, then," he said finally. "A lot depends on her insurance, but I'll have our case manager, Rhonda, get the ball rolling on that and take it from here."

The doctor stood up, and Nicole joined him. "In the meantime, take some time and think it over. What you've offered is not a decision to be made hastily. Sleep on it. We can talk more about it later. It's not a decision that needs to be made today."

Nicole thanked the doctor. He patted her on the shoulder as he stepped out of the room. Nicole sat back down and wondered if she wasn't being rash after all, but even as she wondered, a peace washed over her, and she knew that she had made the right decision.

"Oh, Lord," she prayed, "I'm going to need You more than ever now. There is no way Deborah is going to let me move in and take care of her. I can't wait to see how You handle this."

Chapter 4

The slider door to Deborah's ICU room was shut. Nicole hesitated just a second before she slid it open. She had done a rotation in an intensive care unit during her nursing clinical last fall and was familiar with what to expect. But this was different. This was Deborah, the woman who had opened her arms and heart to Nicole when she and Marc had gotten married. Even though Nicole was probably not the girl she had hoped to have as Marc's wife, Deborah had done her best to make Nicole feel part of the family.

Stepping quietly into the room, Nicole sat down in the high-backed, cushioned chair next to the bed. Deborah lay there motionless, still unconscious. An IV pole stood to one side with bags hanging upside down, pumping the needed medication and antibodies into her. Above Deborah's head, in the other corner, was a screen that monitored her heart. The continuing beeping of her EKG was the only sound to fill the room.

Nicole leaned back into the chair as her thoughts wandered back to the first time she had met Deborah. Marc and she had met at a VA hospital where Nicole had worked and, after a whirlwind romance, had gotten married at a justice of the peace. She remembered how nervous she had been that day when they drove up to meet his parents. It had been awkward at first, but Deborah and Lee had both gone out of their way to make her feel welcome and part of the family.

Marc had been the spitting image of his father, both in looks and personality. They both shared the same quick sense of humor that was often contagious. Nicole's smile dimmed as she thought about Lee. It was hard to believe he was gone. It had been over a year, but Nicole felt his loss strongly, as though it had happened yesterday. It brought her some comfort knowing that Lee had been there to welcome Marc into heaven.

Deborah stirred, and Nicole leaned forward, covering the older woman's hand with her own.

"Deborah," she said softly, "you're okay. You're in the hospital."

Deborah's eyes fluttered open. They were filled with fear and confusion as she focused on Nicole.

"It's going to be okay," Nicole continued. "You've had a stroke, but you're going to be okay."

Deborah's eyes blinked, and she tried to speak, but she had a tube in her throat that wouldn't let her. She tried to grab at the offending tube, but Nicole gently restrained her hand so she couldn't pull it out. The machine let out an alarm. Frustration filled Deborah's face as she glared back at Nicole. A nurse hurried into the room, checked the machine, and then leaned over to check the tube she had tried to pull out.

"You can't be doing that, Deborah," the nurse gently admonished. "I just paged your doctor to let him know you're awake. He'll be in shortly to check you out and determine whether we can take this tube out. In the meantime, you need to be patient and not try to take it out yourself. I know it's difficult, but you'll only make matters worse if you do."

The nurse looked over at Nicole. "Could you give me a minute to get her bed changed and get her cleaned up? I haven't had a chance to do so yet."

"Sure," Nicole said as she stepped to the side and grabbed her purse. "Actually, if you think she'll be okay for a bit, I'd like to go and get freshened up myself."

The nurse assured her that Deborah would be well taken care of until she got back. More than likely, she would go back to sleep as soon as she relaxed and let the medication do its job. Nicole nodded and stepped toward the edge of the bed.

"I'll be back soon, Deborah. I promise."

Deborah opened her eyes slowly. A beeping noise was the only sound she heard. As her eyes adjusted to the dimly lit room, she scanned them over the area, trying to make sense of her environment. A hazy cloud filtered her thoughts, and it took her a moment to register where exactly she was. Just as comprehension came, her eyes came to rest on a figure curled up in the recliner in the corner of the small room.

She knew who it was and yet couldn't recall who exactly. She closed her eyes. She remembered a voice speaking to her. When? Earlier today? Yesterday? Where was she? She wasn't home—that much she knew. She opened her eyes again as she heard noise coming from the recliner. The person stretched and turned toward her, and realization hit her as she recognized who it was.

Nicole? No, it couldn't be!

Deborah squeezed her eyes shut and then looked again. No, there was no mistake. Nicole was here, in her room.

Get her out! Deborah said the words, but nothing came out. The last thing she remembered was stepping outside to get the paper, bending down to pick it up, and then sheer pain screeching through her head. *A stroke!* The words sent terror through her heart. Her mother had suffered a stroke. It had been awful.

God, I don't want to die! she pleaded. *Not like that, please!* Deborah could feel her cheeks moisten as unchecked tears trickled down. She was unable to lift her hand to wipe them away, causing the tears to come even harder.

She saw movement as Nicole stood and came toward her. A tired smile touched her lips but was quickly replaced with concern when she saw Deborah's tears. Nicole grabbed a Kleenex from the small table next to the bed and gently wiped the tears away.

"Shhh …" she whispered, "it's going to be okay. Don't cry, Deborah. You're at Alleghany General. You're going to be okay."

Deborah squeezed her eyes shut, unable to stem the flow of tears that continued to pour out. She heard the monitor start to beep faster and stronger.

"You need to stay calm, Deborah," Nicole soothed. "You're only making it more difficult on yourself."

Deborah heard the door slide open as someone else entered. Nicole and the other person talked in hushed tones, and then the door slid shut again. Nicole returned to her side and once again took her hand. "It's okay, Deborah. They're going to get you something to help you relax."

Deborah's eyes flew open as the nurse walked back in with a syringe.

No, she wanted to protest, but her eyes were already starting to shut as the medicine did its job. She was out before the nurse had finished putting the dose in.

Curled up in a corner recliner, Nicole sat and silently kept watch. Deborah was sleeping comfortably now, had been for the past hour since they had given her the sedative. Maybe it would be a good time to take a break and give Kathee a call.

Standing, she walked over to the nurse's station outside the room to let Deborah's nurse know she was stepping out for a couple of minutes. The nurse smiled up at her and told her to take her time. She reassured her that Deborah would probably be out for a while.

Nicole nodded and quietly left the ICU. She took a deep breath in as she let the door shut behind her. All at once, she felt exhausted. It had been a long, stressful twenty-four hours. Taking her phone out of her purse, she turned it back on as she made her way down the hallway, past a set of elevators, to doors that opened up to an outdoor patio area. Finding the nearest bench, she sat down as she punched in Kathee's number.

Leaning against the back of a park bench, Nicole listened as the phone rang on the other end. She looked around at the bulbs that burst in color along the paved footpath that led to a serene waterfall in a corner of the enclosed area. Tranquil. That was what this garden was meant to make one feel, she thought absently. It helped.

"Hello," Kathee said. "How's Deborah?"

"She's resting now," Nicole said, bringing her focus back to her friend. "She woke up briefly but got so agitated that they had to give her a sedative."

"Well, I've been praying for her and for you. How are you doing?"

Nicole let a smile touch her lips. Kathee was the definitive example of a prayer warrior. If she said that she was praying for you it wasn't just words. She was up every morning a good hour before the boys, spending time in the Word and in prayer. She even kept a prayer journal.

"I know you have. Thanks—we both need it. It's been a tough day." Nicole paused and laid her head back. "I can see the hurt and distress in her eyes when she looks at me, Kathee. How do I get past that?"

"You don't, Nicole," Kathee said softly. "God will take care of her heart. You just take care of her physical needs and leave the rest to Him."

Nicole relaxed as she let her friend's words wrap around her and she felt the peace and strength that they were meant to bring. "Thanks. You're right. I needed to hear that."

"Any time. I'm always here for you. I do know someone who could really cheer you up. Just a minute—let me go get her."

"Okay." Nicole sat up and leaned forward expectantly. A few minutes later, a small voice came on the phone.

"Mommy?"

"Yes, baby, it's Mommy. How is my little buttercup?"

A giggle tickled her ear, and she couldn't help but smile. That little voice washed away all of the exhaustion and pain of the past twenty-four hours.

"Jacob and I are playing. He let me play with his tuck in the sand!"

Nicole smiled at her daughter's animated chatter. "You like playing in the sandbox, don't you?"

There was no reply, but Nicole could see Abby shaking her round face up and down on the other end.

"I get dirty, Mommy. Sand is dirty, but Jacob says it's okay for girls to get dirty. I took a bath, so now I'm clean."

"That's wonderful. Just be sure to obey Aunt Kathee and do what she tells you. Okay?"

"Yes, Mommy. I'm going back outside now."

"Bye, sweetie. Mommy loves you."

"Lub you too. Bye!"

Nicole took a deep breath as she waited for Kathee to get back on the phone.

"Thanks so much, Kathee," she said when her friend got back on. "I really do miss her."

"I know you do, but you don't have to worry about her. She's enjoying her time with the boys, and they are so protective of her. It's like she has three big brothers! We're going to the movies this afternoon. It's supposed to rain, and they all want to see the new Disney film."

"Oh, that's nice. Have fun, and give Abby a big hug and kiss for me."

"Consider it done."

"Thanks. I'll call you tomorrow."

"Sounds good. You be sure to get some rest. You won't be any good to Abby or Deborah if you don't take care of yourself. Talk to you later. Bye."

Nicole closed her eyes and let her thoughts drift back to the day Abby had been born. At the time, Nicole had thought that day was the worst day of her life, but the Lord had turned it into a blessing. That was the day that Kathee had entered her life.

Kathee had been her nurse when Nicole went into labor. She had held her hand and helped coach Nicole through every phase of the difficult labor. When Nicole saw her daughter, she knew something wasn't right. It was Kathee who explained that her daughter had Down syndrome. Nicole had recoiled from the news and refused to hold her daughter.

After two days of Nicole crying and refusing to see her daughter, Kathee had marched into her room with the baby, set her firmly in Nicole's arms, and said, "God gave you this special girl. You should feel blessed that He felt you worthy enough to give you such a gift."

Nicole had just sat there and stared at Kathee, her mouth dropping open with surprise. Then the baby squirmed in her arms, her little fists waving in the air. When Nicole glanced down at her daughter, her heart melted, and tears moistened her cheeks. Looking back up at Kathee, she shook her head and said, "But you don't understand. You don't know what I've done."

"We've all done things we're not proud of, Nicole," Kathee had said. "It's an imperfect world, and we all make mistakes. But this precious child you are holding is not one of them. She's the greatest blessing you'll ever have. Mark my words."

Nicole looked back down at the tiny life in her arms. The tiny, round, flat face with the telltale slanted eyes was suddenly the most beautiful thing she had ever seen. How had she not seen it before? This was her daughter! How could she have ever turned her back on this precious little girl? She looked back up at Kathee with gratitude. This five-foot-three round nurse had opened her eyes to what was important.

"Thank you," she whispered, tears trickling down her check.

Kathee reached for the small box of Kleenex on the nightstand and held it out to her. After Nicole grabbed a handful, Kathee grabbed some too and pulled up a chair to sit next to her.

"It's been a crazy year," Nicole said. "I just didn't think I could deal with a baby, much less one that's going to require so much extra care."

Little fingers reached up and wrapped themselves around

Nicole's index finger. Gently, she rubbed the tiny, short fingers with her thumb. "She is so sweet, isn't she? But you're wrong about me. What I've done does not make me worthy. If anything, if there is a god, this is punishment for what I've done."

"Why do you say that?" Kathee asked softly.

"I was married," Nicole explained, wiping fresh tears away from her cheek. "His name was Marc, and he was a wonderful man. He was in the army, and two years after we were married, he got transferred here. Six months after that, he got deployed a second time to Iraq. When he was deployed the first time, I had his family to help me, but when we moved, I didn't know anyone. After a few months, I got bored and lonely, so I started going out, partying, and having a good time. After a while, I forgot all about Marc. He'd write me emails and call every chance he could, but as soon as we hung up, I was out the door to go hang out and party all night with my friends."

Nicole paused and looked down at her daughter a moment before continuing. "When Marc came home, I was a different person. I'd enjoyed my freedom while he was gone, and I didn't want to give that up. There was no way he was going to keep me from my new friends and life. It caused a lot of friction between us, and we were constantly fighting. After a few months, I told him that I wanted a divorce."

Kathee leaned in and took hold of Nicole's hand, not saying a word. Nicole took in a ragged breath and continued in a trembling voice. "Marc refused to accept that. He fought to keep our marriage together. He was so sweet and loving. He would buy me flowers and make me dinner, but I wanted what I wanted, and I rejected him over and over."

More tears spilled out as she pulled her daughter closer and rocked gently back and forth. "When I think of the pain I caused him … he really deserved so much better. Finally, I moved out when he was at work one day. A friend had offered for me to stay with her, and I thought it was a perfect solution.

"Three months later, Marc served me with divorce papers. Funny, I thought I'd be happy to be finally free, but I didn't feel the joy I thought I would. I didn't feel like I had gotten what I had wanted. I had gotten what I deserved. I signed the papers, put them in the mail, and then went out with my friends to our favorite club to party and to forget."

"I partied hard that night and went home with some guy I had met at the club. I don't remember much from that night. Most of it is still a blur. When I woke up the next morning, the guy was already gone."

Nicole looked down at her daughter as she stroked her angel-fine hair with her finger. "That was the most humiliating experience of my life. I had never done anything like that before. I don't even know his name, or if I did, I don't remember it. I never saw him again after that night, and I was okay with it. I just wanted to put it all behind me, forget it like it never happened. Six weeks later, I started throwing up. I knew before I even took the test that I was pregnant."

Nicole looked up at Kathee with tears of regret in her eyes. "So, you see, I don't deserve this little blessing."

"Nicole," Kathee said softly, "I know this is hard for you to understand, but there is nothing that you have done that God will not forgive. He loved us so much that He sent His Son down here to die for our sins. That debt is paid. All you have to do is believe in Him and accept His love."

"I wish I could ..."

"It'll change your life forever."

"Marc's family are Christians. I went to church with them a few times, but I never got it. I kind of let them think that I believed too, but I was just going through the motions. I wish I had listened better now."

"Don't you have family somewhere?" Kathee asked as she leaned in toward Nicole. "Someone who can help you?"

Nicole shook her head as she spoke. "My mom died when I was six. I don't remember much about her; seems like she was always off with friends, partying. She died of a drug overdose. I never knew who my father was, so my grandma Snelling took me in and raised me. We didn't have a lot, but she did her best by me, and I always knew I was loved."

"Is your grandma still living?" Kathee asked gently.

"Grams died three years ago of a massive stroke. I still miss her so much." Nicole looked down at her daughter, who had grabbed hold of her pinky finger, and smiled. "You're a fighter, I can tell. I think I'm going to call you Abigail."

"That's a lovely name," Kathee said.

"It was Gram's name. Abigail Rose. Yes, that is the perfect name. I want little Abby to always know she is loved."

"Would you like some privacy to get to know your daughter?"

"Yeah, I would like that."

"No problem, honey. Why don't I get back to work so you and your beautiful daughter can get acquainted?"

"Thanks," Nicole said with a soft smile. Kathee stood and squeezed her shoulder as she stepped out of the room.

A warm friendship developed between the two women that day, and they quickly became close friends. Nicole watched Kathee and saw the difference her faith made in her life. When Nicole finally accepted the Lord, Kathee was by her side.

Chapter 5

Nicole inserted the key into the door lock, hesitating just a second before turning it. She felt like an intruder. This house wasn't just Deborah's house. It was her life. All of her dreams, memories, hopes, and pain were in this home. Nicole knew that she was a part of that pain.

Did I ever bring them any joy? she wondered. Maybe at first, after they had gotten over the shock of her and Marc's elopement. It wasn't as though they hadn't tried to include her, make her feel welcome. Some part of her had held back, not willing to accept their love.

She turned the key and swung the door open. Nicole's nose crinkled as she took a strong whiff. There was a smell that she hadn't noticed when she found Deborah lying on the floor that day. It smelled musty, and Nicole didn't think it was just from being shut up a few days. Nicole had a feeling that Deborah had been shut in this house for the better part of six months, maybe longer.

Setting her purse on the small hall table in the front foyer, Nicole made her way into the front living room. The heavy drapes were pulled shut, leaving the room with a gloomy, oppressive feel to it. Nicole walked over to the drapes and pulled them apart to let in the sunlight. Tiny bits of dust particles danced around the paths of the sunbeams. Nicole waved them out of her face as she looked around the room. Definitely needed a good dusting and sweeping in here. Just opening the drapes and letting the sun enter made a world of difference.

Stepping around the couch, Nicole entered the formal dining room. She let her fingertips brush lightly over the large, dark oak trestle table that sat gracefully in the center of the room. The first time she had seen it, she had remarked how beautiful it was. She remembered Marc's father telling her with deep affection how his grandfather had made it for his bride. It had been passed down the family generation after generation, and he hoped to one day pass it down to one of his sons.

At the time, she had hoped she and Marc would one day inherit the lovely table. Nicole hoped that Tyler would appreciate it, but he never seemed one to be the sentimental type, unlike Marc. Nicole let out a sigh as she turned from the table and her thoughts.

Walking over to bay window along the back wall, she pulled up the shades and took in a deep breath. Outside of the window was an explosion of color. Tulips in an array of red, yellow, and white were on display. Unfortunately, it looked like the weeds were overtaking them.

"Another project for another day," Nicole whispered as she turned and walked back through the dining room to the place where she remembered the family spending most of their time. The kitchen had been Deborah's pride and joy. Like his grandfather, Lee had been a carpenter by trade and had built Deborah a kitchen fit for the cover of any home improvement magazine. Dark oak cabinets, light muted granite counters, subway tile backsplash, and a kitchen island that could seat four people comfortably. Next to the kitchen was a cozy breakfast nook with a round oak table and chairs surrounded by windows on all three sides.

The best part was when one turned and looked across the great room at a fieldstone fireplace that reached all the way to the vaulted ten-foot ceiling. Lee had added the family room on, and it was Nicole's favorite room. She remembered lots of happy times in this room with Marc and his family.

Off the other side of the kitchen was Lee's office. Nicole hesitated just a second before turning the knob and opening the door. Immediately, Nicole could tell that this room had not been opened in a long time, probably since Lee's death the year before. She couldn't even begin to understand the depth of Deborah's pain in losing her husband and son in such a short span of time.

Walking across the room, Nicole lifted the blinds and then opened the windows on either side of Lee's desk. A soft breeze circulated the room, sweeping away the musty smell and replacing it with a sweet fragrance. Nicole turned and surveyed the room as an idea raced through her mind.

Deborah's doctor had told her that it would be at least a week before she could leave the hospital. The occupational therapist had been there working with Deborah when Nicole had left earlier that morning. *A week should give me more than enough time to get the house ready,* Nicole mused, *and time to go and visit Abby.* The thought of seeing her daughter again brought a smile to her lips.

With a tug, Nicole finished making the bed in the newly converted den that was off the back. It just hadn't seemed reasonable to keep Deborah upstairs. Not with all the care she would need over the next few weeks or months. The big, heavy desk had been moved out, and a hospital bed had been ordered and placed in what had been Lee's office. It was off the kitchen, and a small bath with a shower stall was right down the hall. It would be perfect for Deborah's needs.

Straightening, Nicole glanced around the room, checking that everything was all set. The ambulance was going to be here in an hour to bring Deborah home. It had been a long couple of weeks. One week had turned into two getting the insurance paperwork taken care of. The hospital had tried getting hold of Deborah's oldest son

Tyler, but his office had stated that he was out of the country working and couldn't be reached. They assured the hospital that they would get in touch with him as soon as they could.

That had been two weeks ago.

"Well, we'll just cross that bridge when we get to it," Nicole mumbled as she took one last look around. Everything seemed ready.

Reaching for her phone, she slipped out to the back patio and dropped into a patio chair. Punching in Kathee's number, she leaned back into her chair and felt the heaviness of the day wash over her.

"Hi," Kathee said, answering on the first ring. "How are you doing?"

"Tired, but as ready as I'm going to be."

"When are you expecting her?"

"In about an hour."

"Want to pray?"

A smile played on Nicole's tired face. She knew that she could always count on her friend to be there for her. She always seemed to know what Nicole needed.

"That would be great," she answered. Then she closed her eyes and listened as, at the other end, Kathee lifted her up to the Lord and asked for His guidance and will for both Nicole and Deborah. When Kathee was finished, Nicole added her *amen* and felt a sense of peace wash over her.

"Thank you," she whispered.

"My pleasure," Kathee said. "I was thinking that maybe you could use a visit from a certain someone. I know you have to be missing Abby terribly."

"Oh, I do," Nicole almost cried. "This has been so hard. I know I got to see her a little over a week ago, but it seems like forever, and it made me realize how much I miss her. I had no idea that this was going to happen when I left or how long this would take me away from her."

"Now, don't start beating yourself up again. Abby has not been a problem, and the boys have been keeping her busy. She's going to have a lot of stories to tell you when you see her."

Nicole laughed at the thought. She couldn't wait to see her precious little girl.

"How about next week? It'll give me time to get Deborah settled and explain about Abby. I'm not sure how she'll take it."

"Would Tuesday work? Matt will be off that Tuesday and Wednesday. He can watch the boys."

"Are you sure you want to make that drive by yourself?"

"Are you kidding? It's only a couple of hours, and it'll be good for Matt and the boys to have some male bonding time. Abby and I will have a blast, just us girls."

"Well, it's more than a couple of hours, but I can't think of anything I'd want more. I so need a hug from my little angel!"

"Well then, it's all set. Abby and I will drive down on Tuesday."

"Great! I'll get the guest room all set for you."

"Well, don't go to a lot of trouble for me. You're going to have your hands busy getting Deborah all settled and adjusting to a new routine."

"I know," Nicole admitted as she worried her lower lip. "I would be lying if I said I wasn't a little nervous about this."

"You'll be fine," Kathee encouraged softly. "Remember that you are not in this alone."

"I know. Thanks, Kathee. Give my little girl a big hug for me, and I'll see you two on Tuesday." Nicole ended her call and threw up a quick prayer for strength.

Deborah could hear Nicole's and the paramedics' voices talking quietly from the front of the house. They had just brought her home from the rehab center at the hospital via ambulance and delivered her home. Seeing Lee's den configured into a bedroom for her was a shock, and even if her vocal facilities were intact, she would have been too dumbfounded to speak. After she got over the shock, she was angry. She listened intently to the voices but couldn't make out what was being said. It was frustrating and a little maddening.

She felt like a prisoner in her own body, and she didn't understand

Nicole. What was her motive? She had been so nice to her since the stroke, visiting her at the hospital and then at the rehab center, taking care of her here. Deborah just couldn't figure out why.

Deborah looked around her new sleeping quarters. Her hospital bed was set up along the wall across from the set of French doors that opened up to the back patio. The windows along the back of the room were open, and a soft breeze floated in. A recliner sat in a nearby corner, and a nightstand was next to her bed. An adjustable hospital bed table stood at the foot of her bed. Everything else—Lee's desk and chair—was gone.

She heard the front door shut and Nicole's footsteps coming down the hallway. Deborah felt herself stiffen. She didn't understand why this had happened to her. Why was she being punished? It was a question that she had been asking herself ever since Nicole's sudden appearance and the stroke.

Nicole knocked softly on the door frame before walking in. "I hope you're going to be comfortable in here," she said.

Deborah looked pointedly to where Lee's desk had been.

"Lee's desk?" Nicole asked, her eyebrows knitted together. "Don't worry—nothing's happened to it. I asked your neighbor's two teenage boys to help me carry it downstairs, along with the rest of Lee's furniture for now. It just wasn't practical to put you upstairs while you're convalescing. This way, you will be able to get around easier as you get better. Plus, you can get outside when the weather warms up."

Deborah managed to let out a huff and turned her face away from Nicole. Maybe she'd get the hint and leave.

She heard Nicole let out a sigh as she walked over to the side of the bed and lightly touched her hand. "I know this won't be easy for you, and I'm sorry you don't like me being here, but it is what it is. I sure didn't plan on this happening, but did you ever consider the fact that this is the Lord's doing? I went back to school to become a nurse, I got saved, and then I felt a strong desire to make amends with Marc and you. It wasn't a coincidence that I showed up on your doorstep three weeks ago."

Deborah could feel her lower lip tremble. She did not want Nicole to see that her words had struck a chord, so she kept her head turned away.

"Okay, then, I'll let you be for now. It's been a crazy morning, and I'm sure you're tired. Why don't you get some rest for a bit before lunch?"

Deborah didn't move until she heard the door shut. Then she couldn't stop the tears.

Nicole climbed the stairs and entered the room that she was using while she stayed there. It was Marc's old room, and it seemed surreal to be there. She could feel him in there, even though the room had been redone since he moved out years ago. Maybe it was just the loneliness she was feeling and a sense of regret that she had never gotten to tell him that she had made a mistake all those years ago.

Had he gotten her letter before he died? she wondered for the hundredth time. What had he thought if he had?

Walking over to the nightstand by her bed, Nicole reached over and flicked on the baby monitor that she had picked up when she went back to visit Abby. It was one that she had used for Abby, and she figured it would help her keep an ear out for Deborah, since she was downstairs.

She heard what sounded like Deborah sobbing on the other end. Sinking onto the bed, Nicole put her head in her hands and wanted to cry too. Instead, she looked up and begged for understanding and healing for both of them.

Chapter 6

Nicole pushed the cart slowly down the bakery aisle of the small, local grocery store. Jeff, the physical therapist, had come by that morning to work with Deborah, so Nicole had taken the opportunity to get out and do some grocery shopping. But if she were to be honest with herself, she just needed an excuse to get away.

The past few days since Deborah had come home hadn't been a picnic. Deborah had fought her on every issue. It was getting discouraging, and Nicole was beginning to wonder if she hadn't made a mistake in staying to help after all.

"I'm sorry, but do I know you?"

Nicole looked up in surprise to see an older, well-dressed lady standing with a cart in front of her. She recognized her as a friend of Deborah's from her church but couldn't place her name.

"Yes," she answered, as she braced herself. "I'm Nicole. Nicole Brennan."

The lady's eyes filled with tenderness. "I'm so sorry. I heard about

Marc. I know you and he were divorced, but it must have been hard on you still. I'm so sorry for your loss."

Nicole was touched and slightly taken aback by the lady's response. Surely, as Deborah's friend, she had to have heard all the awful details about her and Marc's breakup. Why was she being nice to her? Shaking her head, she said, "I'm sorry, but I don't remember your name."

"My name is Gwen Baxter. I'm a friend of Deborah's."

"It's nice to meet you, Gwen. I knew you were a friend of Deborah's—I just couldn't place your name," Nicole said weakly, not sure what to say next. "I'm sorry, Gwen. I'm just surprised that you would even be civil with me after everything."

Gwen looked surprised; then understanding dawned on her face. She leaned over and put her hand over Nicole's. "It's not my place to judge you, sweet child. I've prayed for you during that time and whenever the Lord has put you in my thoughts since."

Tears stung the back of Nicole's eyes as she blinked quickly to keep them at bay. This woman, who had every reason to condemn her, had just told her that she had been praying for her all this time. Words choked in the back of her throat.

"I'm sorry," she said hoarsely. "I'm a little overwhelmed at your kindness. It's been a rough few weeks since I got back."

"Where are you staying?" Gwen asked.

"With Deborah," Nicole responded. "I've been helping her since her stroke."

Gwen looked surprised. "Deborah had a stroke?"

"Yes, I—I assumed you knew."

Gwen shook her head as she spoke. "I haven't spoken with Deborah since Marc's death. It was so soon after she lost Lee that she went into a tailspin. I tried to get through to her, but she completely shut me, and everyone else in her life, out."

"I'm sorry. For her and for you."

Gwen looked at her and said, "Do you have time for a cup of coffee?"

"Sure, I guess so. The therapist will be there another hour yet."

"Good. There's a charming coffee shop that just opened up right around the corner. They have the best strawberry scones. We can talk better there."

A smile touched Nicole's lips. "That sounds good."

An hour later, Nicole was saying goodbye to the therapist after getting his report and instructions on what she needed to work with Deborah on. Deborah had been tired out from the session, Jeff said, so he had put her in her bed for a nap before Nicole had gotten back.

Nicole had looked in on Deborah to make sure she was resting. Seeing that Deborah was resting comfortably, she shut the door with a sigh and went into the kitchen to put the groceries she had gotten away. As she worked in the kitchen, she went over her discussion with Gwen.

She had told Gwen everything about her and Marc, Abby, and her salvation. When she told her how Deborah was rejecting her attempts to reconcile and forgive her, Gwen had just shaken her head.

"Deborah is hurting, but she is also the most stubborn lady I know," Gwen had said. Then she had looked up and pointed her finger at Nicole. "But don't you give up on her. She needs to forgive you as much as you need her forgiveness."

Gwen's exclamation had taken Nicole by surprise. She had never thought of it in that light, and she wondered if maybe there wasn't a little bit of truth in what Gwen had said. When they left, Gwen had promised to come over and see Deborah. Something that was long overdue, she had stated firmly.

Nicole stopped in the middle of chopping the lettuce and shut her eyes. "Thank You, Lord," she said quietly, "for bringing Gwen into my life today. You knew I needed her."

The phone rang, interrupting her thoughts. Wiping her hands on a towel, Nicole walked over and picked it up on the third ring, not wanting to disturb Deborah.

"Brennan residence," she answered.

"Who is this?" the voice on the other end demanded. Nicole

could feel the blood drain out of her face. She recognized the voice on the other end.

Nicole cleared her throat. "It's Nicole, Tyler."

"Nicole!" Tyler stated.

"Yes, Tyler, it's me, Nicole."

"What are you doing there?" Tyler said, his voice lifting in controlled rage.

"I'm taking care of your mother until she gets back on her feet."

"Oh, no, you're not! I want you out of there. Now!"

Nicole went over and sat down at the breakfast table. "Listen, Tyler, I know this isn't ideal, but the only other option is for her to go to a nursing home, and I don't think she would want that. I think that Deborah would do better in her own environment here at home."

"I can afford to pay for her to go to the best nursing facility. How did you get involved in this, anyhow?"

"I was the one who found her when she had her stroke, and I'm more than qualified to take care of her. You may be okay with her going to a nursing home, but what you want doesn't matter. It's what is best for Deborah."

"We'll see about that. I wouldn't be surprised if you didn't cause her stroke! Let me talk to my mother."

Nicole sighed as she shifted the phone to her other ear and said, "Your mother has had therapy all morning and is tired. She's resting now, and I'm not going to disturb her. Besides, Tyler, her stroke has left her unable to communicate vocally, so a conversation right now would only be upsetting for her."

"This is not over, Nicole! You'll be hearing from me again!"

Nicole hung up the phone and took a deep breath. Now that it was over, she found her hands shaking. She had never been good with confrontations.

What Tyler had said about her being the cause of Deborah's stroke weighed heavy on her. In the back of her mind, she had wondered the same thing. She knew stress could be a trigger. Was Tyler right? Had her coming to see Deborah brought on the stroke?

Slowly, she got up and made her way back to the salad that she had started to put together before the phone call. After a couple of chops with the knife, her hands steadied and she was able to breathe. But she had to wonder if she had just made matters worse. Tyler had always been a force to be reckoned with, and it was obvious that he would move heaven and earth to get her gone. She guessed she would have to cross that bridge when she got there.

Right now, all she could worry about was getting Deborah well. She would have to leave Tyler and the rest of it to the Lord.

Chapter 7

The morning fog had been burned off by the afternoon sun. Nicole had just gotten Deborah up into her wheelchair and taken her out to the patio off the den. A little sunshine would do her good. It still felt a little cool after she had taken her out, so Nicole had gone back in to grab a lap blanket to wrap her up in.

She had spent the morning cleaning the kitchen and trying to find the right words to tell Deborah about Abby. She still hadn't figured it out, but she knew that she couldn't put it off any longer. Kathee was bringing Abby to see her tomorrow.

"Here you go," she said brightly as she tucked the lap blanket around Deborah's lap. "That should help keep the chill out."

Deborah had gone from defiant to complacent. Nicole almost wished she were the former; at least then she was fighting. Now it seemed as though she had given up. Nicole pulled a wicker chair around so that she could sit facing Deborah. She wanted to have her full attention.

"Deborah, there is something I need to tell you," she started, searching for the right words. "You see, I have a daughter. Her name is Abby, after my grandma, and she's the light of my life."

Nicole watched Deborah's eyes fill with surprise. Her good arm shook as she slowly raised it and pointed at Nicole. "Marc?" she said slowly.

Tears welled up in Nicole's eyes as she shook her head. "No, Deborah, she's not Marc's. I wish she was, I truly do, but the truth is, I don't know who her father is. I went out the night I got the divorce papers from Marc and met some guy at a club." Nicole looked down at her hands, folded tightly in her lap, as shame crept through her. She glanced back up at Deborah, surprised to see sorrow, not anger, etched on her face.

"Deborah," Nicole said, leaning in, "I want you to know that I never cheated on Marc during our marriage. Not once. I never saw that guy again after that night, and nine months later, Abby was born." Nicole choked back the words as tears formed in the back of her eyes, threatening to overflow. How could she expect Deborah to believe anything that she was saying? Nicole knew that she had broken that trust a long time ago.

Taking a deep breath, she continued. "If it hadn't been for Kathee, a nurse at the hospital, I never would have even held that precious little girl. You see, Abby was born with Down syndrome, and at first, I felt that it was punishment because of what I had done. Kathee made me see that Abby was a gift from God and that He loved me."

She looked up at Deborah and understood immediately what Deborah was thinking. She was thinking of the children Marc would never have, the grandchildren she would never get to babysit, spend the night with, or take to the park. Deborah blamed her all over again. All she had done was open an old wound.

The doorbell chimed in the front of the house. Excusing herself, Nicole went in through the slider and made her way to the front of the house, wiping her eyes on the back of her hand as she went. Her shoulders sagged in relief as she looked through the side window to see Gwen standing on the front stoop. She put on a smile as she opened the door.

"Hi, Gwen," she said. "It's good to see you. Come on in."

Gwen didn't say a word but looked her intently in the face. "What's wrong?" she asked.

Nicole let out a long sigh as she waved her in. "I told Deborah about Abby."

"Oh, I see," Gwen said as she set her purse on the hallway table. "Where is she?"

"She's on the back patio." Nicole put a hand on her arm as Gwen turned to go down the hall to the back. "I opened up her pain all over again."

Gwen patted her hand and smiled. "Why don't you let me have a visit with my old friend? It's been a long time in coming. You look like you could use a break."

Nicole nodded her head as she said, "If you think it'll be okay, I do need to get a few things at the store before Abby and Kathee come tomorrow."

"You go and do what you need to do, and don't worry about us. We'll be fine."

Nicole thanked her again as she grabbed her jacket and purse out of the hall closet and let herself out the front door.

Deborah couldn't get the words out of her head. Nicole had a daughter. The thought filled her with a grief that threatened to tear her apart. A part of her wanted to rage against Nicole, but she couldn't get the words out. Her right arm came up as she knocked the glass off the table next to her in frustration. It hit the flagstaff patio and smashed into a hundred tiny fragments.

"What is all the commotion?" a voice asked from the slider off the breakfast nook.

Deborah looked up in surprise and confusion. That had sounded like Gwen. She hadn't seen her friend since shortly after Marc's memorial, not since she had shut herself away from her friends and her life.

Gwen walked over and stood in front of her, big as life. She surveyed the broken glass that was scattered on the ground around Deborah and then looked at her with concern.

"Are you okay?" Gwen asked as she reached for Deborah's hands and gently looked them over. Satisfied that her friend was okay, she gave her a big hug and then stepped back to look at her more closely. "It's been too long, Deborah. Let me take care of this broken glass, and then we can sit and catch up."

Deborah watched as Gwen strode purposefully back to the slider. A few minutes later, she came back with a broom and dustpan in one hand and the kitchen trash can in the other. After she had swept every last sliver of glass into the dustpan and emptied it into the wastebasket, she marched back into the house. When she reappeared, Gwen had a tall glass of lemonade in each hand.

"Look what I found in the fridge. Lemonade is perfect for a day like today." Gwen set one of the glasses on the same spot where the other glass had sat and gave her a wry smile. "Don't knock this one over now, you hear?"

Deborah looked at the glass that sat next to her. How could she tell her friend that even though she could lift the glass with her good right arm, she couldn't drink it without it drooling down her chin? Nicole always had a straw in it, which made it easier for her.

Gwen went to sit down but caught her friend looking at the glass. Setting hers down, Gwen patted her on the arm and went back inside. A few minutes later, she came back out with a large, red straw.

"I'm sorry about that, Deborah. I saw these in a vase sitting on the kitchen counter when I got the lemonade and wondered why they were there. Nicole is pretty creative, I'll give her that."

She handed the glass so Deborah could grasp it with her right hand and helped her guide it to her lips. After a couple of sips, Deborah handed it back to her, and Gwen set it down on the table.

"How are you doing?" Gwen asked after she sat back down.

"Broken …"

"It's okay, Deborah. It's just a glass, nothing important."

No, not broken … lonely, Deborah thought in exasperation. Why were the words not coming out the way she wanted them to? She hit her hand on the arm of the chair and looked at her friend in frustration.

Gwen leaned forward in her chair, her glass held between her hands. "That's not what you wanted to say, is it?"

"Nooo …"

"It's okay. It will come."

Deborah wasn't so sure. She had never been this dependent on anyone or anything before. Now she couldn't walk, couldn't talk, couldn't do the simplest things! It was humiliating and difficult to accept.

"You know, you don't have to go through this alone, Deborah. Not this stroke, and not the loss of Lee and Marc. You have friends who love you and want to help. I want to help, if you'll let me. But most importantly, you have the Lord."

Deborah stiffened up. *The Lord? Where was the Lord when the drunk driver hit Lee on his way home from a deacon's meeting at church last year, and why did he allow Marc to die in Afghanistan?* No, she couldn't accept that there was a loving God that cared for her. The God she had worshiped and loved never would have brought this on her. Tears streamed down her face, and Gwen put her glass down as she stepped over to put her arms around her friend.

"Don't cry, sweetie," she soothed. "I know it's not been easy for you this past year, and I am so sorry that I wasn't there for you. I never should have let you shut me out."

After a few minutes, Gwen pulled back and gently rubbed Deborah's tears away with her thumbs. "I want to talk to you about Nicole," she said.

Deborah stiffened again and drew herself up in defiance. She was not going to be preached to about that woman.

"Whoa, don't get an attitude with me. I know that look, and it's not going to work on me Deborah Grace Brennan. We've been friends way too long for that."

Deborah relaxed. Gwen was right. She did have a chip on her shoulder when it came to Nicole.

"Nicole and I met at the grocery store the other day. We went out for coffee after that, and she talked. Deborah, I believe she is truly sorry for what she did, and I believe she wants to help you. I think maybe you should give her a chance. From what I can see, she's been nothing but loving and helpful to you." Gwen leaned forward so she could look Deborah in the eye. "If this isn't true and Nicole hasn't been anything but nice to you, I want you to blink your eyes twice."

Deborah knew she couldn't do that. It would be a lie if she did, but how was she going to get past everything that Nicole had done to Marc and to the rest of them? And now she had found out that Nicole had a daughter. A daughter that should have been Marc's! How could she forgive that? *How, Lord?*

Gwen took her hands in hers and held them tightly until Deborah looked her in the eyes again. "Would you like me to pray with you, Deborah?" she asked quietly.

Deborah's eyes teared up as she realized that she did want that. She missed the closeness she had once had with the Lord and with her friend. Slowly, she blinked once. A soft smile crossed Gwen's lips as she bowed her head and prayed.

Nicole slipped into the front entrance and set two large bags on the floor next to her. Shopping had been a nice diversion, but now she wondered how Gwen and Deborah had gotten along while she was gone. Elijah came out of the front room and gently nudged her hand with his nose until she reached down and rubbed his sweet spot behind his ears.

"Hi, boy," she said. "You making sure everyone is playing nice?"

He didn't answer her, just looked up at her with his large, dark eyes and wagged his tail expectantly.

"Well, let's go see how they're doing."

Nicole was pleasantly surprised to see Gwen talking and engaging Deborah in the conversation. Deborah seemed to be relaxed and enjoying the visit. Letting out a sigh of relief, Nicole smiled as she opened the slider and stepped out onto the patio.

"Hi, ladies," she said as she joined them. Gwen looked up and returned her smile, and to Nicole's surprise, Deborah did not look at her with the same loathing as she had before. Her eyes seemed softer and not so judging.

"Well, what good timing, Nicole—I'm afraid I wore this dear lady out," Gwen said as she started to get up. Turning to Deborah, she gave her a hug and a kiss on the side of her face. "Now, you behave and do everything Nicole and your other nurses tell you. I'll be back to visit you tomorrow."

She gave Nicole a warm hug and assured her she could find her way out. Nicole turned back to Deborah and said, "Well, you've had a long morning. How about we go back in, and you can have a nap before the physical therapist gets here?"

"No," Deborah said.

Nicole took a step back. She wasn't sure she had heard Deborah clearly. "No?" she asked.

"Wrong ..."

Nicole looked at her with confusion. Was that not what Deborah had meant? Deborah turned her good hand toward herself and repeated, "Wrong ..."

Nicole sat in the chair Gwen had just vacated and looked intently into Deborah's eyes. "Are you saying that you were wrong?"

Deborah nodded her head slowly.

"It's okay," Nicole said. "I was wrong too. I'm should have found a better way to tell you about Abby."

"No," Deborah said, "It's okay. Want ... to meet ... Abby."

Nicole's eyes glistened as she took Deborah's hands and smiled.

Chapter 8

Nicole threw open the front door as Abby ran up the steps and threw herself into Nicole's open arms. She had been watching for Kathee's car ever since Kathee had texted her that they had hit the city limits. Joy filled her heart as she returned her daughter's tight embrace.

"Mommy has missed my little baby girl so much!"

"I miss you too, Mommy!"

Nicole held her out at arm's length so she could get a better look at her. Kathee had trimmed up her hair, and she wore her favorite Hello Kitty T-shirt with a pair of bright pink shorts. Abby looked back up at her with a huge smile, and Nicole smiled back.

"You lost your front tooth!" she exclaimed.

Abby nodded her head. "It come out when I ate my hamburger. I'm gonna to give it to the tooth fairy."

"Well, maybe the tooth fairy will leave you something for it."

"Jacob says I get ten dollars!" Abby said with wide eyes.

"Wow! Ten dollars?" Nicole said with mock surprise. "I don't know if the tooth fairy carries that much cash with him."

Abby giggled, and Nicole pulled her into another tight hug. It felt so good to have her daughter here with her. Nicole knew that she would have to leave the next day, but she refused to let that thought ruin the time they had together. She was determined to treasure every minute.

"Come on in, you two," she said as she stood. Holding Abby's hand, she reached over her daughter and gave Kathee a big hug. "I can't thank you enough for bringing her, Kathee. You have no idea what this means to me."

Kathee returned the hug and said, "No problem. We had lots of fun on the ride over."

"Let's go into the family room. I want Deborah to meet her."

Kathee nodded, and the three of them started down the hall to the family room. Abby clung tightly to Nicole as they entered the large family area. Deborah sat in a chair next to the fireplace. Gwen had gotten there a half hour before and was seated next to her. She stood and came over to them as they came into the room.

"Well, this must be Abby," Gwen said as she squatted in from her. "It's so nice to meet you."

"Abby, this is Mrs. Baxter," Nicole said. "She's a friend I've made since I've been here."

Abby put her tiny hand out to shake and said shyly, "Hi, Mrs. Baxter."

"You can call me Gwen if you want. You are just so precious!"

"This is my friend Kathee," Nicole added. "She's been watching Abby for me."

"It's so nice to meet you," Gwen said with a smile as she reached over Abby to shake the younger woman's hand. "I've heard a lot about you. Nicole is lucky to have such a good friend."

"Thanks," Kathee said. "It's nice to meet you too."

Taking a deep breath, Nicole took Abby by the hand and walked with her over to where Deborah sat. "Deborah, this is my daughter, Abby."

"Hi … Abby," Deborah said slowly, wanting to get the words out correctly.

Abby studied her intently for a moment and then let go of Nicole's hand to lean forward and give Deborah a hug. Nicole was speechless. In all the scenarios that had played out in her head about this visit, never had she imagined this.

Clearing her throat, she took Abby's hand again and said, "I'd like to show Abby around the house, and then I'll make lunch for everyone."

"I have a better idea," Gwen said. "You go ahead and show Abby the house while I go and get lunch from that deli down the street. You relax and just spend some quality time with your friend and daughter."

Nicole didn't know what to say. Smiling, she nodded and then turned to Abby. "How about, after the tour, I get us some lemonade and we can go sit in the garden?"

Deborah stared out the French doors of the kitchen and watched as Nicole, Kathee, and Abby interacted on the back terrace. It was obvious that Nicole loved that little girl and that Abby thrived under her mother's attention. Deborah could understand Nicole's love. Abby had opened up feelings that Deborah had thought were long gone.

The innocence and love that permeated out of Abby were contagious. Deborah couldn't explain it, but she had felt a peace from deep inside ever since Abby had wrapped her chubby little arms around her and given her a hug. Tears stung the back of her eyes, and she had to pull her attention from what was happening in the backyard.

Gwen had left about twenty minutes ago to pick up lunch from the deli and would be back any minute. It would never do for Gwen to come back and find her like this. She needed to pull herself together before that. Gwen had been reading to her from the Psalms this afternoon, and Deborah felt herself being pulled to the prayers and songs of David. When she started thinking on them, though, a voice in the back of her head always reminded her of what she had lost.

Then her heart would harden again, and she would let herself give in to the anger and despair.

She looked back out at Abby as she chased bubbles that Nicole blew above her head from the bottle in her hand. All three of them laughed as Abby reached her short, chubby hands above her, trying to grasp the bubbles in her hands. Kathee glanced up and caught Deborah watching. Whispering something to Nicole, she stood and made her way inside.

Great, Deborah thought. *She probably wants to sing Nicole's praises. Well, she can save her breath.*

Kathee came in front of Deborah and squatted so they were at eye level. "Would you like to join us?" she asked. "It's a beautiful day."

"No," Deborah said sternly; then she felt sorry for being so abrupt. Rude, actually. That wasn't the way she had been raised or had raised either of her boys. *What has happened to me?* she thought.

Kathee stood to leave. "Is there anything I can get for you?"

"No … thank … you," Deborah replied.

Kathee smiled and lightly touched her shoulder. "I'll head back out, then."

"Lunch is here!" Gwen strode into the kitchen with two large bags in her hands. "Anyone hungry?"

Nicole stood and followed Abby, who bounded in and jumped into a bar stool at the kitchen island, where Gwen was unpacking the bags.

"Did you get peanut butter and jelly?" she asked Gwen as she tried to peer into the bags.

"Yep, and they cut them into squares as per your request," Gwen said as she put the sandwich on a paper plate. "Here's a pickle, chips, and chocolate milk too."

Abby smiled and pulled the plate and glass of milk toward her but didn't make a move to touch the food. Instead, she got off her knees and sat down on the bar stool, watching patiently as Gwen divided the Cobb salad and breadsticks onto four plates and set them on the round oak breakfast table.

Nicole and Kathee went over to Deborah and helped her get

moved from the recliner to her wheelchair; then Nicole wheeled her over so she could sit at the table with them. After everyone was seated, Abby closed her eyes with everyone else as Gwen said grace for their food.

Deborah felt a peace pour over her as she closed her eyes and sent up her own silent prayer of thankfulness.

The next morning, Deborah sat in her wheelchair that Nicole had pushed up to the breakfast table. Gwen had come over with pastries and a flaky piece of strawberry-filled one lay untouched in front of Deborah. She found herself watching Nicole as she chatted with Kathee and Gwen, her hand absently stroking her daughter's fine hair.

Deborah was aware that Kathee and Abby would be leaving soon, and she could sense how hard Nicole was trying to be strong and not let her emotions ruin the little bit of time she had left with her daughter. But Deborah knew.

All at once, the thought of Abby leaving was more than Deborah could imagine. This dear child didn't deserve to be away from her mother, even if her mother was Nicole. It wasn't right. Abby was a sweet, innocent child. She shouldn't have to pay for the sins of her mother.

Deborah looked across the table at Nicole, who had just picked up a fork full of fruit salad to put in her mouth. Nicole stopped midstream and looked at Deborah.

"What do you need, Deborah?" she asked, setting her fork down.
"Abby ..."

Nicole looked at her, confusion clouding her eyes.

"Abby ... stay," Deborah stammered, her eyes never leaving Nicole's.

Nicole could only stare, dumbstruck. Had she really heard Deborah right?

"You want Abby ... to stay?" she asked softly.

Deborah nodded her head. Nicole couldn't hold back the tears. Abby could stay! Never in her wildest dreams had she imagined this scenario. Nicole looked at Kathee and Gwen, who seemed to be as much in shock as she was.

"What's wrong, Mommy?" Abby asked, her lower lip puckering up.

"Nothing's wrong, sweetie," Nicole said as she leaned over and scooped her daughter up. "Everything is perfect."

Nicole looked over the top of Abby's head at Deborah. "Are you sure?" she asked again. Deborah nodded again.

Looking at her daughter, Nicole smiled through fresh tears.

"Mommy crying," Abby said, reaching up to touch Nicole's damp cheek.

"It's okay, sweetie. Mommy's crying because you get to stay here with me! You'd like that, wouldn't you?"

Abby smiled and fervently nodded her head up and down.

Nicole wrapped her arms tightly around her daughter, not wanting to ever let go of her again; then she looked up at her friend.

"I just realized that I don't have anything of hers here. I wasn't prepared for this."

Kathee smiled as she wiped the corners of her mouth and stood up. "Well, it's a good thing that I am." Turning toward Abby, she held out her hand. "Want to help me get your stuff?"

Abby smiled as she skipped over to take Kathee's hand.

Nicole could only stare as she said, "You have her stuff?"

"Call it intuition, but I thought it wouldn't hurt to be prepared in case this was a one-way trip for Abby."

"Oh, Kathee, I can't believe this. This is just so incredible."

"Yeah, I know. Isn't God good?"

Nicole smiled as she said, "Yes, God is good!"

Nicole held Abby in her arms as they waved goodbye as Kathee drove away. They had spent the rest of the afternoon discussing the logistics of what Nicole should do with the rest of her stuff. She finally came to the conclusion that aside from her daughter, there wasn't anything else she needed right then. Abby had outgrown the small toddler bed that she had, and Nicole had planned on picking up a twin bed at a yard sale or on Craigslist anyhow. Nicole had no idea how long Deborah's recovery would take, but Kathee reassured her that the apartment above the garage would be there for her when they came back.

Gwen was wiping down the kitchen counter when they walked back inside.

"You didn't have to do that, Gwen," she said and then added, "but thanks—I appreciate it."

"No problem," Gwen said as she put the dishcloth away under the sink. "Deborah is asleep in her room. It didn't take much persuasion to get her to lie down."

Nicole settled into a bar stool as Abby skittered away to go play with Elijah.

"I'm still in shock over what happened."

"Well, I'm not."

Nicole looked over at Gwen with a raised eyebrow. "You're not?"

"No. This is the Deborah that I remember. I knew she was still in there somewhere. It took that precious little girl of yours to find the chink in her armor."

"Yeah, you're right, but I have a feeling what she did today didn't have anything to do with her changing her feelings toward me."

Gwen leaned over the kitchen island and patted Nicole on the arm. "Baby steps, sweetie, baby steps. Just give her time. The Lord is working on her."

"I hope you're right," Nicole said with a shrug. "I guess only time will tell."

Chapter 9

The next week was a whirlwind of activity as Nicole got Abby situated at Deborah's. She decided to put her in Marc's old room, which had a twin bed in it, and moved herself across the hall to the master suite.

Now that things were getting settled, Nicole had another decision to make. She really wanted Abby to get socialized with other kids. Abby had had that at the church they went to along with Kathee's three boys, and Nicole didn't want her to lose that. Nicole finished making her bed and was heading across the hall to check on Abby's progress with her room when the doorbell rang.

"Come on, Abby," she called as she started down the stairs. Nicole was nearly knocked down when Abby plowed by her a few seconds later in a rush to get to the door. By the time Nicole reached the bottom step, Abby had the front door open.

I really need to talk to her about "stranger danger," Nicole mused as she joined her.

"Gwen!" Abby exclaimed as she jumped up and down in place.

"Hi, pumpkin!" Gwen said as she bent down to give her a hug before walking in. "Hi, Nicole! How's everything going?"

"Fine," Nicole said as she closed the front door and led them to the back of the house. "The physical therapist is with Deborah now. Abby and I were just upstairs cleaning our bedrooms up."

"How's the physical therapy coming?"

Nicole gave her a tight smile and said, "Slowly."

Gwen paused and thought for a moment; then she twirled her finger in the air as she said, "You know what Deborah needs? She needs to get out of here for a while. What do you think?"

"A picnic sounds wonderful. There's a nice park just up the road that would do. Deborah has about another half hour of therapy left. That should be more than enough time to throw it all together."

Abby was pulling at Nicole's jeans. "I want to go to park!" she exclaimed.

Nicole laughed. "Yes, you can go too."

"Good, that's settled," Gwen said as she headed back to the kitchen.

"We'll have Jeff show us how to get Deborah in and out of the car," Nicole added. "I think between the two of us we can handle it okay."

"Sure we can, and if we drop her a few times, maybe she'll get mad enough and learn to do it herself!"

Nicole chuckled. "That would definitely get her motivated."

An hour later, they were seated at a picnic table under a large elm tree. A gentle breeze carried the sweet fragrances of lilacs that had just opened up. Nicole pulled out the turkey sandwiches she and Gwen had thrown together, along with chips and a large container of potato salad they had picked up at a small grocery store along the way. Abby sat on a large blanket with a dolly and some other toys she had brought with her.

Deborah watched as she sat in her wheelchair at the end of the table that was specifically designated for handicapped use. She hadn't said a word when Gwen and Nicole announced their plans, though she wasn't so confident of Nicole and Gwen's ability to lift and move her from the car to her chair, but they had done it without a hitch.

If she were to be honest, it did feel good to get out of the house for a bit. Inadvertently, she let out a soft sigh and felt herself relax. Therapy had been especially rough this morning, and she wasn't sure how much more she could endure. Especially when she didn't feel like she was making any progress, even though her therapist, Jeff, told her she was doing well. It would just take time, he had said this morning.

Time, she thought. She'd had way too much of that for too long now. A butterfly flitted by, and she found herself mesmerized at the beauty of it. Deborah remembered the beautiful flower gardens she had tended in her yard for so many years and all the butterflies and hummingbirds that been drawn to her flowers. She used to so enjoy sitting in her backyard and enjoying nature.

Suddenly, Deborah wanted that back. To feel the joy and love and to live again, not just exist. A resolve bubbled up inside of her, and she felt a purpose in her life again. She was tired of feeling sorry for herself and watching life slide by. Lee and Marc wouldn't have wanted that for her either. They would be so sad if they could see her now.

Nicole came and sat by her so she could help Deborah with her food. Deborah placed her right hand on Nicole's as she scooped up a forkful of potato salad for her. Nicole looked at her with a raised eyebrow. Deborah squeezed her hand tightly.

"Is everything okay?" Nicole asked.

Deborah shut her eyes. She knew that if she was going to get better, it had to start from the inside. She opened her eyes and looked Nicole unwaveringly in the eye.

"Do you want something else?"

"No … this … perfect. Thank … you."

Tears welled up in Nicole's eyes as she answered. "It's no problem, Deborah. I want you to know that I do love you."

This time Deborah didn't hide the tears. *Lord,* she prayed, *help me to forgive her.*

"Looks like our picnic was a success," Gwen said as she helped Nicole pack up. "I haven't seen Deborah this relaxed in a long time."

"Yeah," Nicole mused. "She did seem like she was enjoying herself. I know Abby had a good time. I would like to get her into a daycare. Someplace that could help her a little more."

"I should introduce you to Kim Johnson," Gwen said as they walked the short distance to her van to load the picnic supplies. "She goes to our church, and she is the special education director for our school systems."

"Really?" Nicole said. "That would be great!"

"Why don't you and Abby come to church this Sunday, and I can introduce you?"

"Sure, let me see if I can get someone from the agency to come and watch Deborah."

"Good. That's settled. Now let's get the rest of the gang here and head home. I bet you will have two people ready to take a nap this afternoon."

Nicole smiled as she said, "Make that three."

Gwen chuckled as she turned to head back to where Deborah and Abby waited. She grabbed Abby's hand as Nicole took control of Deborah's wheelchair, and together they got both of their charges loaded and situated for the short ride back.

Gwen stayed and helped Nicole get Deborah in bed. By the time they were finished, Abby had fallen asleep on the couch in the front room. Nicole grabbed a comforter and tucked it around her daughter. She smiled up at Gwen and then motioned for her to follow her to the kitchen.

"Do you want a glass of iced tea, or do you need to take off?"

Nicole asked as she opened the refrigerator and reached for the container of tea.

"I would love a glass of iced tea," Gwen answered. "It's not like there's anyone waiting at home for me."

Nicole gave her an inquisitive look over her shoulder.

Gwen paused and then shrugged her shoulders. "Sorry, I don't usually indulge in self-pity."

"That's okay," Nicole said as she poured two tall glasses of tea and handed one to Gwen. "We're all entitled to a little self-pity every now and then. Even you."

Gwen followed Nicole into the family area and sank down at one end of the couch. Nicole settled into the chair across from her and took a sip of her tea.

"I really have no complaints, mind you," Gwen said as she ran the tip of her finger around the rim of her glass. "I have been blessed in so many ways."

Nicole paused before asking, "I don't know your entire story, Gwen, just tidbits that I've heard. If you don't want to talk about it, that's fine. But if you do, I'm a good listener."

"You're referring to Hal," Gwen said quietly.

Nicole nodded and relaxed back in her chair, giving Gwen the space she needed.

"Hal and I met my senior year of high school," Gwen began. "He was the football jock, and I was the head cheerleader. No one was surprised that we hooked up. We were inseparable that year and only had eyes for each other. That fall, Hal asked me to marry him. He was getting ready to leave for the university upstate, and I was planning on going to the local community college here. I said yes, and we planned a big wedding for when I finished my degree in two years. Then I would move upstate with Hal while he finished his schooling.

"We had it all mapped out," Gwen continued. "It seemed like a perfect plan. I was in love and naïve. I believed in happily ever after, but there is no such thing. At least, not for me."

"What happened?" Nicole asked.

"I really couldn't pinpoint it exactly, but Hal started to change.

I could feel him pulling away as the date got closer. I'd ask him if everything was okay at school, with us. He was always quick with that smile of his and assured me that everything was fine. I just figured it was the pressure of school and finals, so I brushed it off. But in the back of my mind, I knew something wasn't right."

Gwen paused as the memory washed over her. "Two weeks before the wedding, Hal got expelled from school for cheating. Seems he and a buddy found a way to hack into a professor's computer and steal the test answers for the final. They sold the answers to other students, and it was one of them that turned them in."

"That had to be so difficult for you."

Gwen just looked at Nicole and gave her a wry smile. "Oh, that wasn't all. I forgave him, and we continued with the wedding plans. I figured we'd get through it together and all would be fine. Looking back, I see how naïve I really was. Two days before the wedding, I got a call from some girl informing me that she and Hal had been seeing each other for quite some time. Of course, I didn't believe her, but when I confronted Hal, he didn't deny it. He just hung his head, and I knew that my whole life up to that point had been based on a lie."

"Gwen," Nicole whispered, "I'm so sorry."

"Don't be," Gwen said, shaking her head. "It was for the best, really. When I think what life would have been like if I had married Hal, I thank the Lord every day that He intervened."

Tears sprang up in Nicole's eyes as she looked over at Gwen. "I don't understand why you don't hate me after what I did to Marc. It had to bring all those feelings back up."

Before Nicole knew it, Gwen was up and over to her in three quick steps. She threw her arms around Nicole and engulfed her in a hug.

"Grace," she whispered in Nicole's ear. "It's the same grace God showed me; how could I not show it to you too?"

Nicole buried her head into Gwen's shoulder and cried as Gwen soothed and rocked gently back and forth. After a minute, Nicole gently pulled away and wiped her eyes with the backs of her hands.

"You know, I've heard about God's grace, but until this moment, I never really understood it." Nicole looked up at Gwen. "Thank you."

"No thanks needed, honey. I've learned over the years to have no regrets. Besides, I've heard through the grapevine that Hal just got remarried for the third time. All in all, I consider myself quite blessed."

Nicole chuckled at that as they both stood.

"I think I need to head out," Gwen said, picking up her purse. She threw an arm around Nicole's shoulder as they headed up the hall to the front. They took a quick peek at Abby, who was still asleep on the front couch, before heading to the front door. Gwen turned as she opened the door. "See you Sunday?"

"We'll be there," Nicole said as she gave her a quick hug.

Nicole closed the door quietly behind Gwen and then leaned against it, sending up a quiet prayer of thanks.

Sunday morning was busy, getting both her and Abby ready and out the door as soon as help showed up to watch Deborah. Nicole managed a sigh as she leaned back in the driver's seat and let herself relax. It had been weeks since she had been able to make it to a church service, and she found herself excited to be going again. Quietly, she wondered if the services had changed since the last time she had been here with Marc. The thought saddened her, but she managed to shake herself out of it. Marc would be overjoyed that she was going.

She pulled into a lot that was filling up fast. She got Abby out of her car seat, and they walked up to the front door of the church hand in hand to find Gwen waiting for them with a smile.

"Hi, you two!" she exclaimed. "Don't you both look beautiful!"

Abby smiled up at her and reached up for a hug, which Gwen gave freely.

"Come on, I'll take you back to the children's wing." Gwen looked back at Nicole and added, "You can meet Kim. She and her husband, Tom, are in charge of the children's program."

Nicole could only nod and follow Gwen as they wove through people and hallways to the children's wing. A petite lady was standing at the doorway to the room where Gwen was stopped and leaned

65

down to talk to Abby. Gwen pointed to something on the inside of the room, and Abby scurried in. Nicole was surprised that Abby didn't hesitate.

"Nicole," Gwen said, turning to her, "this is Kim."

Nicole took Kim's outstretched hand in hers. The smile Kim offered reached her eyes, and Nicole immediately felt comfortable.

"Hi," she said. "It's nice to meet you."

"Same here," Kim replied. "That must be Abby. Gwen has told me all about her. She seems like a sweet little girl."

Nicole laughed. "Well, most of the time. I can't complain though. She usually is very good."

"Gwen says that you would like to get her registered in preschool?"

"Yes, I really want to get her acclimated to life here and to other kids her age."

"That is a really good idea," Kim agreed, "and the school system here has a really good program for kids like Abby that will both be nurturing and give them the life skills they need. I got some leaflets I brought with me that you can take home and browse through if you want."

"Yes, that would be great," Nicole said, excitement welling up inside of her.

"Good. Let me go and grab those for you real quick."

Kim disappeared into the room and returned a moment later with a handful of leaflets.

"Take a look at these and let me know what you decide."

"Thanks," Nicole said. "I will let you know as soon as possible."

"Great, and if you have any questions, feel free to give me a call. My number is on the back."

Nicole thanked her again and then let Gwen guide her back to the main auditorium for the service. The auditorium had already started to fill up as they grabbed a couple of seats toward the back. On stage, a band was warming up, and within minutes, everyone was on their feet and lifting their voices of praise to God.

Nicole enjoyed the music and the feeling of love that resonated in the air. She had to admit, it felt good to be in church again. The feeling of being uplifted and close to God among other believers was something she had missed since everything had begun with Deborah. She was absorbed in the pastor's message that morning on Philippians and found herself yearning for more when the message was over and everyone stood up to leave.

People she didn't know came up to greet her. For the first time in a long time, Nicole felt like she was home, and the knowledge settled warmly in her chest as she smiled and shook hands with those around her.

Chapter 10

Telling Gwen how much she had enjoyed the service, Nicole promised to do her best to be back the next Sunday. Abby hadn't stopped chatting since she picked her up, and continued all the way home.

She smiled at her daughter in the rearview mirror as Abby told her over and over about her new friends and the stories the teacher had told about a boy, David, who threw some rocks at a giant and killed him. She clutched papers to her chest that she said she had drawn for Mommy and Deborah.

It touched Nicole that her daughter had thought to do a picture for Deborah. She hoped it would make Deborah feel as good as it did her. They were still laughing and talking as they pulled into the driveway. Nicole got out and went to the other side to unhook Abby from her car seat. Abby was still chatting about Sunday school as they made their way up the walk to the front door.

Nicole turned the handle and entered, calling out, "Lisa, we're back."

Lisa came down the hallway, a worried expression on her face.

"Hi," she said in a soft whisper. "I'm glad you got back when you did. A guy showed up, said he was Deborah's son."

Nicole stopped dead in her tracks and stared at the girl in front of her.

"Tyler?" she asked.

"Yeah, I think so. I thought it would be okay for him to come in, but now I'm not so sure. He's been very … disruptive. He's saying all sorts of things, getting Deborah all upset. I wasn't sure what to do."

"That's okay, Lisa," Nicole reassured. "I'll take care of it from here."

"Okay," Lisa said as she grabbed her bag and made a quick exit.

Not knowing what else to do, Nicole took Abby's hand and walked down the hall to the family room. Every step of the way down the long hallway, she sent up a prayer. She entered the room and turned to face Tyler, who stood by the fireplace, glaring at her.

"Hi, Tyler," she said as confidently as she could. "I didn't know you were coming today. Can I get you some coffee or tea?"

"Don't worry about that," he spat at her. "I won't be long. I'm on my way to China for business and had a layover, so thought I'd stop by. I think it would be best to get Mom into a rehab center. I've had ones in the area checked out and have found one that can get her in right away."

Nicole glanced over at Deborah, who was sitting rigid and tight-lipped in her wheelchair. Turning to her daughter, she bent down and spoke softly. "Abby, honey, I want you to go outside and play with your toys for a little bit while I talk with this gentleman."

Abby looked warily at Tyler. For a moment, Nicole didn't think she would leave, but Abby let go of her hand and walked over to Deborah. Silently, she put the picture she had drawn for Deborah in her lap and then headed out the French door to the back patio. Nicole watched as her daughter sat down at the small picnic table she had bought for her and started to play with a set of Lincoln logs. Satisfied that Abby was out of earshot, Nicole turned her attention back to the problem at hand.

"Tyler, there's no need to do that," Nicole said. "I've already explained that I am all set to stay here and take care of Deborah. Both the case worker and her doctor agreed that this would be the best place for her to heal and get better. Can't you see that this is obviously upsetting your mother?"

Tyler planted his hands on his hips and glared back at Nicole. "I know what you're up to. You say that you are doing this out the goodness of your heart, but I did some digging. You're getting paid to help my mother. That's why you're doing this, not because you care."

Nicole let out a soft sigh before answering. "I am getting paid because that's how it was set up through the hospital, but I promise you, I am not getting rich taking care of your mother. It covers expenses but nothing more. Trust me, I would make a lot more working as a nurse than as an aide like I am now. I am here because I care."

"I don't believe you," Tyler said. Then he pointed out the window to Abby. Nicole could see the revulsion in his eyes. "And you are not going to get away trying to pass *that* off as my brother's!"

Nicole glared back at Tyler. "Her name is Abby, and you will not degrade her in front of me again!"

"Oh, yeah?" Tyler sneered. "Tell me, what name is on her birth certificate?"

Nicole could feel heat rising up her neck to her face. She did not feel like she needed to defend her choices to the man standing in judgment before her, but she raised her head high and answered his question anyhow.

"Her full name is Abigail Rose Brennan."

"I knew it," Tyler said as he stabbed his finger at Abby out the window. "You planned on pawning *that* off as my brother's."

Fury wrapped itself around her, and she was ready to recoil and lash out at the man in front of her when a voice raised itself from behind her.

"Stop!"

Both Nicole and Tyler looked over in surprise to Deborah.

"Tyer," Deborah slurred as she pointed her good arm at her son. "You have … no say. My life … still. I want … them … to stay. Here."

Tyler stared at his mother, and Nicole silently wondered if he would listen to Deborah. Finally, he threw his arms out to his side.

"Fine, my Uber car will be here any second to take me back to the airport. I don't have time for this." He threw another glance at his mother before turning to Nicole. "This is not over. You've wormed your way into my mother's house somehow, but don't get comfortable. I'll figure out your scam."

He walked over and planted a kiss on Deborah's cheek before storming down the hallway to the front door. Nicole followed and peered out the front window to see him get into a car that was pulled up in the driveway. She walked back to the family room and sat next to Deborah.

"Tyler … gone?" Deborah asked.

"Yes," Nicole answered as she put her hand on top of the older woman's. "Are you okay?"

Deborah was visibly shaken still, but she managed to give a weak nod.

"I am so sorry," Nicole said.

"Didn't … raise him … like that," Deborah said with a slow shake of her head.

"I know you didn't. I saw your example in Marc."

Deborah's lips raised in a sad smile. "Yes … Marc."

"I think you've had enough excitement today. Do you want to go sit outside with Abby while I get lunch? It's real pretty out there today."

Deborah nodded her head in silent agreement. Nicole paused before standing to push her out.

"About Abby," she began. "I want you to know that at the time, I couldn't think of any name that I would have been more proud of my daughter to have than Brennan. I still feel that way. I hope you are okay with that."

Deborah smiled and lifted her good hand to reach over and cover Nicole's. "I … am … happy she … is … a Brennan … too."

Tears welled in Nicole's eyes as she leaned over and pulled Deborah into a deep hug. She pulled back as another thought hit her. "Deborah, I just realized something. That's the most words I've heard come out of your lips since your stroke. You're making progress!"

Realization hit Deborah too, and she gave Nicole a wry smile.

"Mo … ti … vation," she said.

"Maybe," Nicole agreed, "but I got a feeling the Lord had a hand in it. He gave you your voice when you needed it to stand up for Abby and for yourself.

"Come on," she added as she got behind and started to push Deborah's chair out through the patio door. "I think we should have lunch on the patio. It's way too nice to be inside. I'll get you situated, and you and Abby can hang out while I throw something together. Then we can all relax and enjoy the afternoon together."

Nicole watched them out the window over the sink as she rinsed off the vegetables she was getting ready to chop and serve with dip. The sandwiches were done and all set on plates ready to go, but she had needed a few more minutes.

Tyler's visit had shaken her more than she had let on to Deborah. Deep down, she wondered about his agenda. He was like a pit dog when he got his teeth into something and wasn't one to let go. She knew this wasn't over. Not by a long shot.

She took the vegetables over to the chopping block, deftly sliced the peppers up, and then diced some broccoli and cauliflower. She added them to a platter that had tomato wedges that she had already cut up on it. She put a small bowl of vegetable dip in the center and smiled with satisfaction at how pretty the arrangement looked.

Why am I letting Tyler get to me? she thought. *He's going to do what he's going to do. I just need to trust that the Lord has this under control.*

With a new resolve, Nicole decided that she was not going to let Tyler ruin any more of her or anyone else's day. Adding the vegetable platter to the tray that already had the chicken salad sandwiches for her and Deborah and a peanut butter and jelly sandwich for Abby on it, Nicole picked the tray up and headed out to where Abby and Deborah were sitting.

As she joined them, she found herself humming a song they had sung that morning in the church service. She smiled as she remembered His promise that the words of the song had conveyed.

Chapter 11

Deborah watched as Abby sat in the chair across from her and read a book quietly to herself. She could tell by how Abby ran her fingers under the words that she was concentrating hard on what they said. Nicole had decided to set them in the living room after breakfast because she said it caught a lot of the morning sun.

Looking up, Abby saw Deborah watching her. She slowly climbed off her chair, walked over to where Deborah sat on the couch, and climbed up next to her.

"Why can't you walk?" she asked Deborah, her eyes filled with curiosity.

Deborah thought how best to answer the child so that she would understand but not be scared. "I got … hurt … I fell," she answered slowly.

Abby mulled that over for a moment. "Will you get better?" she asked.

"Maybe … hard work."

"You should ask Jesus to help you. That's what I do when something's hard. He always helps me."

Deborah looked down at the child, who looked up at her with such innocence. How wonderful it would be to have the faith of a child again. She had had that faith at one time, a long time ago, before life got in the way.

"Who ... told you ... about Jesus?" she asked.

"Mommy."

Deborah wasn't surprised at the little girl's answer. She had seen Nicole's faith played out over the weeks she had been here. There was no denying that Nicole had changed, and now Deborah knew that it was real because Nicole had told her daughter about Jesus.

"Want me to read to you?" Abby asked as she opened a book in her lap. Deborah could see that it was a children's story about Jonah.

"Yes," she answered slowly. "I ... would like ... that ... very much."

Deborah listened attentively as Abby read from the small children's book about Jonah and the whale, her stubby little fingers running under the words as she went along. When she struggled with a word, Deborah found herself helping Abby sound it out the best she could. When they finished a couple more books, Abby grabbed the last one in her stack and looked up at Deborah.

"You read this one," she requested.

"Okay," Deborah agreed as she pushed back the butterflies in her stomach. So far, even though she had been compliant with the speech therapist, she had not felt like she had made much progress in moving forward. Tyler's visit and threat to move her into a nursing home had both scared and angered her. She was even more determined than ever to do whatever it took on her part to make progress in her recovery and get out of this prison her body was currently bound in.

Smiling at Abby, she opened the book and followed along as together they read the story aloud. When one of them stumbled, the other was there to help the other along. Deborah felt a deep sense of accomplishment when they finished the story.

"You did good," Abby said as she looked up at her with a smile.

"Yes, you both did." Nicole stood in the entranceway, a smile touching her lips. Walking over, she reached over and mussed Abby's hair with her fingers. "Almost time for lunch. You girls hungry?"

"Yes," Abby said, her eyes dancing with excitement as she added, "and then the bus will come and take me to school!"

"Why don't you go get washed up? And then we can eat."

Abby nodded her head as she jumped off the couch. She grabbed the armful of books and marched up the stairs.

Nicole let out a soft sigh and then turned and smiled at Deborah. "I should probably go help her, or no telling what she'll pick out to wear. Abby has quite an eclectic taste when it comes to her wardrobe, and not in a good way, I'm afraid."

Deborah watched as Nicole followed Abby upstairs to her room. *Her room,* Deborah mused. When had it stopped being Marc's room? She had a sense that Marc would be pleased that his room that had once held GI Joes and army tanks was now home to Barbie dolls and a pink Barbie convertible.

She had to agree.

"Hold still, Abby. I can't get your arms in your jacket if you don't." Nicole continued to wrestle with Abby and the jacket as the small bus pulled into the driveway and honked. Abby was out the door with Nicole still trying to get the coat on her. She finally had success just as the bus driver swung the door open, and Abby quickly clambered up the three steps into the bus, waving at Nicole as she made her way into her seat.

Nicole stepped back and waved at her daughter through the window, but Abby was already chatting with another child next to her and didn't notice her mother anymore. Nicole continued to wave and watch until the bus had disappeared down the road.

Turning, Nicole made her way back into the house and shut the door with a sigh. It was obvious that preschool was going to be harder on her than on Abby. She walked into the living room, where Deborah sat looking out the front window. She stood next to her and peered out the window to where the bus had disappeared down the road.

"Abby … will be … okay," Deborah said.

"Yeah, but will I?" Nicole asked. "Being a parent is hard."

"I … know," Deborah answered.

Of course she does, Nicole thought. Stepping behind Deborah, Nicole reached down to unlock the brakes on the wheelchair.

"Jeff will be here soon," she said as she started pushing the chair down the hall. "He's going to show me some things I can do to help so I can work with you more in between his visits."

"Great … more … bosses," Deborah complained half-heartedly.

Nicole chuckled as she rolled the wheelchair into the family room. She maneuvered the wheelchair over by the fireplace before locking the brakes. Walking around in front of Deborah, Nicole bent over so she was looking her straight in the eyes.

"Well, if you want to get rid of us, then you need to get fighting mad and start getting serious about this recovery. You're the only one that's holding you back."

Deborah didn't flinch as she met Nicole's gaze, and Nicole saw a resolve in Deborah's eyes that she hadn't seen before.

She lightly tapped Deborah's leg and said, "That's more like it."

Chapter 12

"I'm coming," Nicole muttered at the continued beckoning of the doorbell. Elijah trudged along next to her as she hurried from the back of the house to answer the door. She assumed it was Jeff, the physical therapist, but why he hadn't let himself in like he usually did after the first ring was a mystery to her. The doorbell rang again just as she pulled the door open.

"Jeff, why didn't you ..." The words got lost in her throat as Nicole came to a stop.

It was not Jeff who stood in front her but a complete stranger. A young man with short cropped hair, wearing a pair of worn blue jeans and a gray T-shirt, stood awkwardly on the stoop staring at her.

"Can I help you?" she asked, as she got hold of herself.

"Yes, ma'am," the young man said. "I'm sorry to disturb you. I'm here to see Mrs. Brennan."

Nicole was still at *ma'am*. Really, he called her *ma'am*? Where was he from? Shaking her head, she looked up at him, finally understanding what he had said.

"Do you mean Deborah?" she asked.

"Yes, ma'am."

Oh, he really has to stop that, she thought.

Elijah let out a whimper as he sat at her feet, his tail sweeping the floor behind him. The stranger smiled and leaned down to rub the dog behind his ears.

"This must be Elijah," he said with a soft smile.

"I'm sorry. I don't mean to be rude, but who are you?" she finally asked.

"Sorry, ma'am," he said, appearing to be apologetic, "my name is Reese Taylor. I served with Mrs. Brennan's son, Marc."

Nicole felt the blood drain out of her face. Reese quickly reached for her, putting his right hand under her elbow to steady her.

"Are you okay, ma'am?" he asked, concern etched on his tan face.

"Yes, I'm sorry. It was just a surprise, that's all." Nicole regained her composure and gestured for Reese to come in. It was then that Nicole noticed the cane he held in his left hand.

"If you don't mind, I'll have you wait in the living room here while I tell Deborah you're here. I'm afraid this will be a surprise for her as well."

Reese followed Nicole into the living room but elected to stand in the middle of the room. He gave her a questioning look as he leaned on his cane.

"I'm sorry," Nicole said, knowing she owed Reese some sort of explanation. "Deborah had a stroke recently. We were actually expecting her physical therapist. That's who I thought you were." Nicole realized she was rambling and stopped.

Reese cocked an eyebrow at her and said, "I'm very sorry to hear that, ma'am."

"Let me go and see if she's up to a visitor." Nicole turned to leave but paused at the hall entrance. She turned to look back at Reese.

"And please, don't call me ma'am," she said. "My name is Nicole. I was Marc's wife." Quietly, she turned and left, Elijah at her heels.

Reese didn't move from his spot in the middle of the room as he watched Nicole leave the room and head to the back.

"Nicole?" he said under his breath.

He had seen a picture that Marc carried of her, but he hadn't expected to find her here, at Marc's home. She didn't look quite the same. There was something different about her, something he couldn't put his finger on. He realized that the picture Marc had shown him was old, but it was more than how she looked. The picture he had seen of her was the picture of a girl ready to take on the world.

A party girl, Reese thought.

At least, that had been his first impression. He and Marc had been buddies since boot camp and had done three tours together in Iraq. He considered Marc like a brother. It was Reese whom Marc had called when things had gone south in his marriage after they got back home from their second deployment. He knew how devastated Marc had been when Nicole had left him and how badly he had wanted to save his marriage.

He had been there to support Marc when it fell apart, leaving his best friend broken. He had done everything he could to help his friend put Nicole behind him and move on with his life. As far as he had been concerned, the girl was certifiably crazy to walk away from a man like Marc. Marc was a stand-up guy that deserved better than what he got.

What he couldn't wrap his head around was why she was here. That made no sense. Reese shook his head as he walked over and lowered himself down on the edge of the sofa. He wasn't prepared to deal with her now. He was here to see Marc's mom, and he needed to keep focused on that.

Slowly, he raised himself back up when he heard Nicole come back into the room. Her expression was drawn and tight as she said, "Deborah would like to meet you."

Reese nodded as he stood and started to follow her. Nicole stopped him before he took a step.

"She's been through a lot, and she is still weak from the stroke," she said softly. "I don't know how much she will be able to take."

Reese looked at Nicole and was surprised at the compassion and concern that he saw radiating from the depths of her eyes. He felt conflicted as he nodded again and followed her to the back of the house. He didn't know what to expect and was beginning to wonder at the wisdom of coming here. He didn't want to cause Marc's mother any pain; he just wanted to bring his condolences and tell her how much Marc meant to him.

He kept his face from registering the shock when he saw Deborah. The lady in front of him looked frail and tiny sitting in the wheelchair. He walked over to her and gathered her small hand in his.

"It's a pleasure to meet you, Mrs. Brennan," he said with respect. "My name is Reese Taylor, and I had the privilege of serving with your son in Iraq. Marc was a special guy and a good friend. I considered him a brother."

Tears welled up in Deborah's eyes as she looked up at him. Her lips quivered as she smiled and covered his hand with her own.

"It's … a … pleasure … to meet … you, Reese," she said. "Marc … talked highly … of you too."

Reese motioned to the footstool next to her and asked, "May I?"

Deborah nodded her head and motioned for him to sit down. Nicole took a seat at the end of the couch, far enough away to give them space, but close enough if Deborah needed her. Reese sat down and folded his hands neatly in his lap.

He paused and took a moment to gather his thoughts. There was so much he had wanted to say, but now he wasn't sure what would give her peace and what would give her more pain. He turned his attention back to the lady sitting in front of him. Deborah looked expectantly back at him.

"Marc talked a great deal about you and his father," he said, keeping his voice soft. "I know that he thought of you and his father often and missed you both terribly. I was with Marc when he got news of his father's death. He took the news hard."

Deborah's lower lip quivered, but she kept her eyes focused on Reese. Reese looked down at his hands a moment before raising his gaze back up to meet Deborah's.

"When he came back from his father's funeral, he had something with him. It belonged to his dad." Reese reached into his pocket and pulled a handkerchief out. He laid it in the palm of his hand and slowly opened it up. "I thought that you might like to have it back."

Deborah let out a small gasp when she saw the Purple Heart medal lying in the middle of the handkerchief. She looked up at Reese with surprise.

"Marc was proud of his dad," Reese continued as he picked up the medal. "He told me how his father had saved the men in his unit in Nam when they came under attack. How he held off the enemy and risked his life to save them. That was why Marc joined the army. I think he took this because he wanted a piece of his father with him over there."

Reese held the medal out toward Deborah, who had lost any effort to keep her composure. Tears ran unabated down her cheek, and she was unable to control the quiver in her lip. Out of the side of his vision, Reese could see that Nicole was unable to hide the tears either.

"I think you should have this back," Reese said as he laid the medal gently in her hands. "You are a very blessed woman, Mrs. Brennan. Marc and your husband were both brave men."

Deborah sobbed openly as she wrapped her hand around the medal and brought it up to her chest. Nicole was at her side in a heartbeat and wrapped her arms around the older woman as they cried together. Reese sat back and gave them a moment. Finally, Nicole looked up and wiped the tears from her eyes.

"You don't know what this means. To both of us. Thank you."

Reese nodded, feeling uncomfortable. Stiffly, he stood up and grabbed the cane leaning against the chair next to him.

"I'm going to get going. I didn't mean to bring you more sadness, Mrs. Brennan. I just thought you would want to have that back."

"Yes, you were right," Nicole said. She looked down at Deborah, who smiled through her tears and reached a shaky hand out to Reese.

"Thank ... you," Deborah said.

"You're welcome, ma'am," he said as he took her hand.

"Let me show you out," Nicole said as she stood. She turned back to Deborah and said softly, "I'll be just a moment, okay?"

Deborah smiled and nodded her head before giving Reese's hand a squeeze and letting go. She turned her attention back to the medal as they made their way out of the family room. Elijah ignored them and went to lie at her feet.

They were silent as they made their way to the front door, both lost in their own thoughts. Nicole stopped him with a hand on his arm as Reese stepped through the door,

"Thank you for that," she said. "It means more than you can ever know."

"I know that she's lost a lot over the past year," Reese said as he looked Nicole in the eye, "and I can understand that."

"Will you be here long?" Nicole asked as she leaned into the door. "I think Deborah would like to see you again. I'm sure she would like to hear more about Marc's time over there."

"Just waiting to get my discharge papers finalized," Reese answered as he looked down at the cane by his side. "I'm hoping it will only take a few more weeks, but you never know with the military."

Nicole followed his gaze. "I'm sorry," she said. "Did ..."

Reese interrupted her before she could finish. "Yes, I was injured in the same attack."

Nicole reached over and touched his hand. "I didn't mean to pry. Please come back. We would really like to see you again before you leave."

"I'll do my best," Reese said. Nicole nodded and released his hand.

Turning, Reese made his way slowly down the walk and got into his car. As he pulled away, he glanced up at Nicole, still standing in the doorway. She lifted a small hand and waved goodbye. He turned his attention back to the road, but his mind was in turmoil.

Nicole was not what he had expected.

Reese reached into the inside pocket of his jacket and pulled out a long envelope. On the front of it was Nicole's name, written out in Marc's cursive handwriting.

"What do I do with this now?" he asked himself.

Chapter 13

"Look at you!" Jeff stepped back as he watched Deborah take a shaky step forward, her hands gripping each side of the walker. "Keep this up and you'll be doing marathons in no time!"

Deborah grunted and said, "Be happy to ... make it ... across room."

Jeff laughed as he walked slowly next to her, ready to step in and help if he saw her starting to falter at all. "You're doing great. I'm really impressed with the progress you've made the last few weeks."

Deborah didn't respond as she concentrated on putting one foot in front of the other. It might seem like progress to Jeff, but Deborah was not having any of it. Nothing but a complete recovery was going to be acceptable, and this was a long way from that. She had never been one to step back from a challenge, and she wasn't going to let this beat her.

"Okay, Deborah, why don't we turn and head back to your recliner?"

Deborah made the slow pivot with the walker to turn back the other way and slowly made her way back across the family room to her chair. She pivoted the walker again and eased herself back down into the recliner. She settled back with a satisfied sigh.

"Well, you should be pleased with yourself, Deborah," Jeff said with a smile. "You did very well your first time with the walker."

"Want to … show … Nicole and … Abby," Deborah said pointing down the hall.

Jeff glanced at his wristwatch. "I think that is a good idea. They should be back any time."

"Hey, Jeff, we're back!" Nicole's voice carried down the hall as the front door opened and closed. Deborah glanced up at Jeff, her eyes round with anticipation and a little fear.

Jeff patted her arm as he stood to make his way to the front of the house. He met Nicole and Abby by the front stairs.

"Is everything okay?" Nicole asked, concern etched in her voice.

Jeff waved his arm with a shake of his head. "Everything is fine. Deborah did very well. As a matter of fact, she has something she wants to show you, so if you would give me a second before you come back?"

Nicole looked at Jeff and nodded. Jeff smiled and turned, making his way back down to the back. She mused over his behavior as she took her own and Abby's jackets off and hung them up in the front closet.

"Okay, you can come now," he yelled finally.

Nicole smiled down at Abby and shrugged her shoulders. Together, they walked down the hallway and entered the family room. Nicole's eyes lit up and Abby clapped her hands when they saw Deborah standing with her walker. Abby started to run to her, but Deborah stopped her.

"No … wait. I want … come to … you."

Abby stopped dead in her tracks and watched with keen interest as Deborah made her way slowly to her. When she reached Abby, Deborah stopped and smiled down at her. Abby laughed and wrapped her arms tightly around Deborah's legs.

"You did it, Gramma! You did it!"

Deborah and Nicole looked at each other, stunned. It was the first time Abby had called Deborah that. Nicole's eyes grew wide, wondering how Deborah would react.

She watched as Deborah's eyes went from surprised to moist. Quietly, she bent over and returned Abby's hug.

"Yes, I did," she said softly. "Your gramma ... loves you ... very much."

Tears choked the back of Nicole's throat as she watched the scene in front of her. Abby had called Deborah *Gramma*, and Deborah hadn't batted an eye.

Recovering, Nicole stepped forward with a smile. "That was remarkable, Deborah! You should be very proud of yourself."

"Thank ... you," Deborah said as she looked up over Abby's shoulder.

"Okay, Miss Deborah," Jeff said, slinging a workout towel over his shoulder. "That's enough showing off for now. Let's get you back to your chair. We don't want to overdo."

Deborah clucked her tongue as she let go of Abby and started the process of turning the walker around.

"*We* didn't ... walk all ... the way across ... the room," she said, throwing her nose in the air as she made her way back across the family room.

Jeff chuckled as he guided her back and helped her into the recliner. As soon as she was seated and comfortable, he moved the walker out of the way. Squatting next to her, he said, "No more of the walker tonight, you hear me? You've had quite an afternoon and have made a good deal of progress. I don't want you to hurt yourself. I'll be back Thursday, and we can work on it some more. Okay?"

Reluctantly, Deborah nodded her head.

"Good. I'll see you same time on Thursday."

Nicole stepped forward with a quilt and wrapped it snuggly around Deborah's lap as she said, "Thanks, Jeff."

A few minutes later, they heard the front door shut as Jeff let himself out.

"Gramma, I get book for us to read?" Abby asked, her eyes shimmering with excitement.

Nicole looked at Deborah and saw her eyes were heavy. She leaned over and touched Abby's soft, round cheeks and said, "I think Grandma needs a nap, honey. She's had a busy morning. Besides, it's your naptime too.

"Do I haf to?" Abby whined.

"Yes, you do. If you take a nap same time as Grandma, then you can read with her after you both get up."

Abby mulled that in her head as her tongue rolled from one side of her mouth to the other. Finally, she shook her head and smiled as though it was a great idea. Nicole sighed with relief that it wasn't going to be the battle she had expected.

"Deborah," she said, turning back to face her, "let me get li'l pumpkin here settled, and I'll come back and take care of you."

"Take ... time," Deborah said, her eyes nearly half shut. "I'm okay ... here."

Nicole wasn't surprised to find Deborah snoring away when she came back down a few minutes later. With a smile, she decided to make good use of some free time. She grabbed her book that was on the end table and headed to the slider. Seemed like a good time to go enjoy some downtime in the backyard.

Later that night, Nicole made two cups of tea for her and Deborah before joining Deborah in the family room. She carefully handed the cup to Deborah; then she walked over and curled her feet under her as she nestled down into the couch. She sighed as she wrapped her hands around the warm mug and took a long sip.

"Is Abby ... all tucked in?" Deborah asked as she blew softly into her hot cup.

"Yes, finally," Nicole said as she closed her eyes and leaned her head back. "It only took three stories and a promise to go to the zoo this weekend."

"She got you wrapped ... around her little finger."

"You should talk," Nicole shot back with a smile.

Deborah chuckled. "You're right ... hard not to. She's a ... precious little girl."

A comfortable silence filled the room as they worked on their tea and watched the fire that Nicole had turned on in the gas fireplace. Nicole felt a peace and thankfulness that Deborah had come to love her daughter. Was it possible that the Lord was using Abby to open Deborah's heart to forgiving her?

"I hope ... we see ... Reese again," Deborah said, her eyes staring reflectively into the fire. "I would like ... to hear more ... about Marc ... but Reese seemed ... lost."

"I know. I got the same impression," Nicole said as she took another sip. "I've been praying for him. He seems like he is searching for something—I don't know what, but I'd like to help. I'd like to do it for Marc."

Deborah looked over at her, surprise written all over her face, and said, so softly that Nicole almost didn't hear her words, "I want to pray ... for Reese too."

Nicole sat up, looking Deborah in the eyes for a moment. Then she reached over and gently took the older woman's hand in her own. Quietly, they shut their eyes, and each took a turn lifting Reese up in their prayers.

Chapter 14

"Come on, Abby! The bus will be here any minute!" Nicole yelled up the stairs, her hands planted on her hips in frustration.

"Comin'!" Abby's muffled voice came from upstairs.

Nicole shook her head as she started up the stairs. No telling what her daughter was doing. Last week, she had come downstairs in her Cinderella gown from Halloween.

"Abby!" she yelled again as she got to the top of the stairs.

"I'm here," her daughter said as she stepped out into the hallway, nearly bumping into her mother. Nicole groaned as she saw the red lipstick Abby had attempted to put on her lips. Mostly, it went from one cheek to the other. She spun her daughter around and headed to the bathroom.

"What were you doing in Mommy's makeup, young lady?" she admonished as she grabbed a wet washcloth and began to wipe it off.

"I want to look pretty ... like you, Mommy," Abby said as she stood still and let Nicole scrub her face until it was rubbed clean.

Nicole set the washcloth down and squatted back down in front of her daughter. Gently, she took Abby's face in her hands. "You know that you are beautiful just as you are. You are my perfect little girl."

Abby smiled and then quickly squirmed away as they heard the bus honk its horn.

"Bus here!" she squealed as she ran from the bathroom. Abby was halfway down the stairs before Nicole could catch her.

"Hold on a minute," she said as she grabbed a jacket out of the hall closet. "You may need this. Give me a kiss."

Abby quickly kissed Nicole on the cheek before running out the door and climbing into the small bus that was waiting for her. Nicole stood out on the front porch and waved to the bus driver, Loraine, as the bus door shut. She watched as the bus carefully backed out and then turned to go back inside when she heard a horn honk. A smile touched her lips as she saw Gwen pull into the driveway.

"Hi!" she said as Gwen got out and made her way up the sidewalk. "Was Deborah expecting you?"

"No, I was in the area doing some errands and decided I would stop by for a minute." Gwen had a smug smile as she held up a plastic grocery bag. "I just happened to stop by Rick's grocery store and pick up a coffee cake to go along with our coffee this morning."

Nicole smiled and slipped her arm through Gwen's as they stepped inside. "Well, Deborah will be delighted that you did. Wait until you see the progress she's made. It's amazing how far she's come in the last few weeks."

"So you said when we talked the other day. Can't wait to see it for myself."

"Who's there, Nicole?"

Nicole smiled at Gwen's expression as she saw her friend push her walker slowly down the hallway toward them.

"Well, look at you, missy," she said, her eyes lighting up. "You've been busy since the last time I saw you."

Deborah's eyes were full of pride as she walked over to her friend and then reached up and gave her a warm hug. They hung onto each other for a few seconds before Gwen broke away and looked at Deborah.

"You look good," she said.

"Why don't we head back to the family room?" Nicole said as she took the coffee cake from Gwen. "You two can talk and get all caught up while I get this coffee cake cut up and get the coffee going."

"Sounds like a plan," Gwen said as she down on the sofa.

"Yes, sounds good ... to me too," Deborah agreed.

Nicole watched her as Deborah made her way back to the recliner. It was hard not to step in to help, but she knew that Deborah needed to do this on her own. She let out a soft sigh as Deborah settled back in the recliner before walking over to the kitchen island.

"I see that I just missed Abby," Gwen said as she sat her purse on the floor next to her feet.

"Yes, and you missed seeing me having to scrub bright red lipstick off her face just before the bus came," Nicole stated as she took the coffee down from above the stove. She put a coffee filter into the top of the coffeepot and carefully scooped the coffee into it.

"She didn't!" Gwen laughed.

"Her face was scrubbed raw by the time I got it all off."

"She ... is full ... of it," Deborah said with a shake of her head. "You have ... your hands full."

"Don't I know it," Nicole said with a sigh.

As the coffee brewed, she pulled out three small plates and dished a generous piece of coffee cake onto each one. A few minutes later, she brought Deborah and Gwen each their coffee and cinnamon roll. They thanked Nicole as they took their plates and coffee from her.

Nicole walked back to the island, grabbed her piece of cake and coffee, and then returned to her seat. She carefully set her cup of coffee down on the small end table so she could take a bite of the coffee cake.

"This is so good!" Nicole exclaimed. "Thanks for stopping by and picking this up for us, Gwen."

The phone rang before Gwen could respond.

"I got it!" Nicole licked her fingers as she rose to answer the phone.

"Hello," Nicole answered, still licking her fingers. Suddenly, she stood straighter; the voice on the other end had her full attention. "Accident! When? ... Where? ... Is Abby okay?"

Gwen set her plate down on the coffee table and looked over at Nicole, concern etched in her face. Deborah put her coffee on the end table next to her and leaned forward anxiously.

"Yes," Nicole said into the phone as she grabbed a slip of paper and a pen off the counter and started to scribble notes on it. "Mercy Providence. Got it."

"What's going on?" Gwen asked as Nicole set the phone back down.

"Abby?" Deborah asked as she leaned forward.

Nicole's face was ashen when she turned toward them. "That was the school. There was an accident—Abby's bus was sideswiped at an intersection."

Both Gwen and Deborah gasped at the same time. Gwen quickly rose to go stand by Nicole. Nicole looked frantically around the room.

"I need to get to her! I need my keys. Where is my purse?"

Gwen stepped next to her and laid her hand on her arm. "You are in no condition to drive. Let me take you."

Nicole looked from Gwen to Deborah; then she shook her head as she said, "Thanks, but I need you to stay here with Deborah."

Before either of the ladies could protest further, Nicole hurried up the hallway to the front door. Gwen followed her and found her searching frantically through her purse, which she had found on the hall table.

"Found them," she said as she held the keys up in front of Gwen. "I'll give you a call as soon as I know anything."

"Nicole, please wait. You won't do Abby any good if you have an accident too."

"I'll be okay," Nicole reassured her as she pulled the front door open.

"Whoa, where's the fire?"

Nicole took a step back in surprise. "Reese! I didn't hear you!"

Reese took one look at Nicole's frantic face and put his hand up. "What's wrong, Nicole?"

"It's Abby! She's been in an accident, and I need to get to her!" Nicole started to go around him, but with one look at Gwen's pleading eyes, Reese put his arm out to stop her. He gently turned her toward him and looked her squarely in the eyes.

"Let me take you to your daughter," he said softly but firmly. "You're in no condition to drive."

Nicole looked as though she was going to argue but suddenly relented.

"You're right," she agreed. "Do you know how to get to Mercy Providence?"

"No, but the rental car has a Garmin in it. That will get us there quickly."

Reese turned and nodded to Gwen as he shut the door. Gwen walked over to the front living room window, pulled the curtains back, and watched as they got in Reese's car and backed out of the driveway. A few seconds later, his car was a speck in the road as he took off. Gwen blew out a breath and said a quick prayer for Abby and Nicole.

Once they were out of sight, Gwen dropped the curtains back and let out another deep sigh. She turned around to head back to Deborah, only to find her friend standing in the entranceway to the living room, a look of determination shooting darts across the room at her.

"What?" Gwen asked, walking over to where Deborah stood.

"I'm going ... too."

Gwen shook her head. "Deborah, there's nothing you can do there. It would be best just to stay and wait to hear from Nicole."

"No!"

Gwen stopped in her tracks and looked with surprise at Deborah. She had not heard such determination come from Deborah in a long time.

"I am going ... if I have ... to push this walker ... all the way!"

"Well," Gwen said, "guess I better get my coat and keys, then. It'll be much faster if I drive you."

"Gwen," Deborah said as her friend walked around her. Gwen stopped and raised an eyebrow at her. "Thank ... you."

Gwen smiled and patted her shoulder as she continued up the hallway to retrieve her purse and keys. A few minutes later, they were both seated in Gwen's car and backing out of the driveway.

Chapter 15

Nicole drummed her fingers nervously on the ledge of the reception desk counter as she waited for the receptionist to get off the phone. She had worked a rotation in ER last summer, but it was a whole different thing being on this side of it. Finally, after what seemed an eternity, the receptionist hung up and turned back to her, a soft smile on her lips. Nicole leaned in anxiously.

"If you go to the door, I will buzz you in. Michael is your daughter's nurse. He will meet you and take you to your daughter."

Nicole quickly thanked the girl as she grabbed her purse and headed over to the set of double doors that were opening up. She swung by where Reese had been standing off to the side. She slowed long enough to let him know that she was headed back to see Abby.

"I'll wait out here," he said quietly. Nicole nodded her head and touched his arm in thanks as she continued through the open door.

A tall, stocky man with a shock of red hair pulled back into a short ponytail met her on the other side of the open door. He looked like he belonged in a wrestling ring inflicting pain, not in an emergency room helping to heal pain.

"Hello, Mrs. Brennan," he said softly. "My name is Michael. I'm Abby's nurse. Your daughter is just down this hall."

Nicole followed Michael as they headed down the hall to a cubicle that was partitioned off on three sides with a multi-blue curtain. As they walked down the hall, Michael filled Nicole in on her daughter's condition: "Seems when the van was struck, it threw Abby out of her seat on the small bus. Luckily, the SUV hit on the other side of the van from where Abby was seated." Michael warned Nicole of what to expect, but she already knew.

Nicole took a deep breath as Michael pulled back the curtain for her to enter. She could not hold in the gasp that escaped her as she saw her daughter lying on the bed in front of her. She looked so pale and small in the bed with the IV in one arm and the monitors bleeping above her. The left side of her face was swollen and black and blue.

"We will be taking her down to x-ray shortly," Michael said quietly as he reached over to adjust her monitor. "They want to be sure nothing is broken, but I think her guardian angel was watching over her. Considering everything, I would have to say that she's a very lucky little girl."

Nicole leaned over and gently stroked the side that wasn't bruised. "Abby, Mommy's here."

Abby looked up at her mother with glassy eyes and then shut them.

"They gave her something to relax her, so she's a little out of it," Michael explained.

Nicole nodded as she continued to gently stroke her daughter's face.

"Thank You, Lord," she whispered as tears brimmed over in gratitude.

The curtain parted, and two techs appeared to take Abby for her x-ray. Nicole stepped aside as they made sure all IV bags and monitors were secured before they released the brakes on the gurney and rolled Abby gently out of the cubicle. She was relieved that Abby seemed oblivious to what was going on.

"Can I come?" she asked.

"Sorry," Michael said as he stepped next to her.

"I'm a nurse," Nicole interjected. "I can handle it. I've handled much worse."

Michael shook his head as he took her arm and moved her away from the moving gurney. "It's hospital policy. Your daughter will be well taken care of, I promise you. You can wait here if you like, or you can go to the waiting room. I will let you know when she's back."

Nicole watched as the gurney made its way down the hallway with her daughter on it. When it disappeared through the double doors at the other end, she turned to Michael.

"How long will she be?"

"It shouldn't take no more than twenty minutes," Michael assured her.

Nicole absently nodded her head as she looked back down the empty hallway where her daughter had been taken.

Michael gently touched her arm and said, "I will let you know the minute she gets back."

"I want to wait here for her."

"That's fine. Can I get you a coffee?"

Nicole shook her head no.

"Is there anything I can do for you?"

Nicole looked up at him and gave him a soft smile. "You've been more than helpful, Michael. Thank you, but I'm fine right now."

"Okay, but if you need anything, just holler."

Nicole sat down in the chair next to the empty spot where Abby had lain just a few minutes before. Relief and fear pitted themselves against each other in the bottom of her stomach. All the *what ifs* fueled the raging battle within.

What if Abby had been seriously hurt or worse? Nicole pushed those thoughts back. She couldn't let them take control. Her daughter was fine, and she thanked the Lord again for that. She suddenly remembered that she had left Reese out in the waiting area. Picking up her purse, she stood and looked outside the cubicle for Michael.

Finally, she spotted him coming out of another curtained room and walked quietly over to him. She explained that she had to go back out to the waiting room for a few minutes but would be right back. Michael promised to come get her if Abby returned before that. With that reassurance, Nicole shouldered her purse and pushed her way through the double doors that led back to the waiting room.

The ER had filled up quickly since she had left Reese, and it took her a few minutes to scour the room for him. She finally found him hunkered down in the back corner, his cane propped on a chair next to him. He had his arms resting on his legs with his head bent over, staring hard at the floor.

Nicole suddenly realized how hard this had to be on him—the noise, the confusion of everything going on around him—and her heart went out to him. She knew a little bit about PTSD, and she had wondered more than once if Reese might be suffering from it. Seeing him now seemed to confirm that diagnosis. She made her way through the wave of people to where Reese held his vigil and sat down on the edge of the lone empty seat next to him.

Reese looked up when he felt her next to him and asked, "How is Abby?"

"Abby is fine," she reassured him. "She's having an x-ray right now to see if anything is broken. She looks pretty bruised and beat up, but other than that, I think she looks good."

"That's good to hear," he said, relief washing over his face, and Nicole was touched by his concern.

"Thanks again for bringing me, Reese. You have no idea how grateful I am," Nicole said, "but there's really no reason for you stay. This is going to take a while. They may have to run more tests to check her all out, and I don't plan on leaving her side any time soon, so you might as well take off."

"Are you sure?" Reese asked as he looked at her with concerned eyes. "I can stay as long as you need. It's no problem."

Nicole shook her head before he was even finished. "I appreciate that, Reese, I really do, but it's not necessary. If you could stop by and check on Deborah for me on your way back, I would really appreciate it. That would help take a lot of stress off me right now. Just let her know Abby's okay and that I will give her a call later. I know she's worried, and I'm concerned about having to leave her like that."

"Where's … Abby?"

Nicole turned her head in surprise to see Deborah coming up next to her, seated in a wheelchair. Gwen stood behind her, sheepishly grasping the handles.

"Deborah!" Nicole cried as she leaned over and wrapped the older woman in a warm hug. It was a gesture that surprised her—and, judging by the expression of shock on Deborah's face, one that surprised her too. "What are you doing here?"

Determination glinted from the older woman's eyes. "I came … to see … about Abby."

Nicole looked imploringly at Gwen, who had reached down to pull the levers on either side of the chair to lock the wheels up.

"Don't look at me," Gwen stated as she straightened back up. "Deborah was determined to get here, even if she had to push that walker all the way by herself. I've known this lady for thirty years, and I have no doubt she would have done just that. I didn't think either of us wanted that on our conscience," she added with a raised eyebrow.

Nicole just shook her head as she leaned forward to take Deborah's hands in her own and wondered how she had gotten so blessed.

"Abby is fine," she said, looking Deborah in the eye. "She is off having an x-ray right now to see if there are any broken bones. She's a little bruised and beaten up, but other than that, we have a very lucky girl whose guardian angel took very good care of her today."

"Amen," Gwen said.

Tears filled Deborah's eyes and she pulled her gaze away from Nicole, but Nicole gently pulled her face back to hers and then wrapped her arms tightly around the older woman again,

"It's okay, Deborah," she whispered in her ear. "Abby is fine."

After a few minutes, Deborah pulled away and reached into her coat pocket. Pulling out a worn Kleenex, she dabbed it under her eyes, trying to get her composure back.

"I'm … sorry," she said. "I … was just so … worried."

"No need to apologize, Deborah. Thanks for caring enough to come here. It means a lot to me that you care about Abby so much. I know that little girl thinks the world of you."

"I … love that … precious little girl."

The simple words hit Nicole hard, and she had to suppress fresh tears as she folded Deborah in another warm hug.

"She loves you too," she whispered in her ear. Deborah softly patted her on her arm as she pulled away.

"Mrs. Brennan."

Nicole straightened up and saw Michael standing in front of her. "Is she back?" Nicole asked.

"Yes, she is. Dr. Phillips is with her and would like to speak with you as well. He asked me to come and get you."

"Okay." Nicole stood and turned to the others sitting around her. "I'll be right back."

Nicole followed Michael back to Abby's cubicle. She wanted so badly to ask him what the test results showed, but she knew he wouldn't be able to tell her. That was why the doctor was waiting for her, and deep down, fear gnawed at her stomach. The x-ray had to have shown that Abby did have a broken bone—why else would the ER doctor be waiting to see her?

Michael pulled back the curtain to Abby's cubicle, and Nicole stepped in. Abby was still asleep, thankfully. At least she wasn't feeling the pain right now. The ER doctor who had been taking care of Abby stood at the head of her daughter's bed.

Nicole had been in such a panic when she had first gotten there that she hadn't been able to focus much on what was going on around her. She hadn't been able to grasp exactly what the ER doctor had to say about her daughter. All she had cared about was that Abby was okay.

Now she saw that Dr. Phillips was tall and lean, like a runner, with just a touch of grey framing his face. The smile he gave her went all the way to his eyes, and Nicole immediately felt relaxed around him. He motioned for her to have a seat in the chair next to Abby; then he pulled out a stool, rolled it in front of her, and took a seat so that he was level with her.

"We did an x-ray to check out your daughter's left arm," he began, setting the clipboard with Abby's chart on his knees. "When we first examined Abby, her arm was swollen and tender. She also had a difficulty rotating it. That made us suspect that it might be broken, and the x-rays we did confirmed that."

"What kind of fracture?" Nicole asked as she took her daughter's good hand in her own and gently massaged the top with her thumb.

"The type of fracture she has is called a physeal fracture," Dr. Phillips explained as he leaned forward. "It's located in the growth plate, which is in the radius bone near the wrist." He held up his arm and pointed to the area on his own wrist. "We will need to get a cast on that right away. They will be taking her down to do that soon."

Nicole nodded as she continued to rub her daughter's hand. She turned to look down at her daughter, who continued to sleep, oblivious to all that was going on around her. For that, Nicole was thankful.

"We are also concerned about a possible concussion from her being thrown around the bus during the accident," Dr. Phillips continued, "so between that and her wrist, we would like to admit Abby for a day or two for observation and a few more tests."

Nicole choked back the fear that crept up her throat before turning back to the doctor and slowly nodding her head in agreement.

"Of course," she said. "Whatever is best."

"Good, I'll have the staff start the process, and we'll get Abby comfortable and feeling better soon." Dr. Phillips stood and gave Nicole an encouraging pat as he stepped out. Nicole heard muffled voices, and a few seconds later, Michael stepped back into the cubicle.

"I hear we're going to have a guest for a few days," he said pleasantly. "First, though, we are going to take care of that arm and get a cast put on it. What's Abby's favorite color?"

Nicole didn't even hesitate with her answer. It was an easy one. "Purple."

"Perfect!" Michael said with a broad smile as he rechecked all the wires and monitors. "That's my favorite color too! Purple cast it shall be!"

Nicole threw him an appreciative smile. He was doing his best to help her relax through the process, and she appreciated it, but she couldn't help but worry.

Michael glanced sideways at her as he got Abby ready to be taken down for her cast and said, "I had a sister who broke her arm when she was about Abby's age, and within no time, she was out running around and behaving as though nothing had happened. Most kids are very resilient. Abby will be back to her old self before you know it."

Nicole smiled over at Michael. "Thanks, I do know that. It's just so much harder when it's your child."

"They should be here shortly to take Abby for her cast. I'll let you have a few moments with her alone until then. If you need anything just push the button on the side of the bed."

Nicole smiled her thanks and leaned forward as Michael quietly left them alone. Pushing Abby's bangs back, Nicole silently thanked the Lord for His protection over her daughter and for a quick and complete healing.

Chapter 16

Deborah fidgeted in her wheelchair, silently cursing her inability to get up and walk on her own two feet back to where Nicole and Abby were. Of course, she knew it wasn't the wheelchair holding her back. She just wasn't accustomed to being so helpless to take care of herself and, more importantly, helpless to take care of Nicole and Abby.

Most annoying of all, she hated not knowing what was going on behind the far doors. She stared at the double doors on the other side of the busy waiting room and willed them to open and let Nicole walk through them with news on how Abby was doing. This waiting was not in her DNA. She had always been one to react and cause things to happen. When had she become so compliant?

On cue, the doors swung open, and Nicole walked through. Deborah could see the dark shadows under Nicole's eyes as she made her way through the mass of people who were all waiting to be seen or to hear news of their loved ones. Nicole seemed oblivious to everyone else as she made her way over to where they sat waiting.

Deborah felt Gwen grab her hand and squeeze it tightly with quiet reassurance.

Nicole reached them and gave them a feeble smile as she sat on the edge of a nearby chair. "Abby's arm is broken," she explained softly. "They are putting a cast on her arm now, and they are going to keep her an extra day just for observation. They want to make sure she doesn't have a concussion either."

"Was she awake?" Gwen asked.

"No, she was still pretty medicated. It's a blessing, really. She isn't feeling any pain right now."

"That's good," Deborah said and then leaned in to cover Nicole's hand with her own.

Nicole looked at her, and a smile touched her lips at the gesture. She turned to the rest of them and said, "There's really no need for all of you to hang around here. There is nothing any of you can do right now. I already told Reese that I would be staying here with Abby, so why don't you all go back home? If anything changes, I will give you a call."

"Don't you want to run back home and get a change of clothes?" Gwen asked.

"No, I'll be okay for one night. I really don't want to leave her."

"I want to … stay with you." Deborah stated firmly.

Nicole looked over at her with bright tears and squeezed Deborah's hand that still held hers.

"That means more to me than you can know," she said, "but there really is nothing you can do." Nicole turned to Gwen and asked, "Could you stay with Deborah? I would feel so much better if she weren't alone tonight."

Gwen was nodding her head before Nicole was finished. "Of course I can. I had already planned on doing that."

Deborah shook her head. When had she become such a burden? Abby needed them. It was then that Deborah realized that she needed Abby too. In the short time that they had been in her life, Abby had come to mean the world to her. She turned pleading eyes back to Nicole.

"Please," she begged. Nicole looked at her, and Deborah saw the turmoil running through her head as to what to do.

"I have an idea," Gwen interjected. "How about Reese drops me off at Deborah's? I'll grab a few things for Nicole, throw them in a bag, and drive Nicole's car back here. That will give Deborah time to spend with Abby, and when I come back, I can take her back home in my car. That way, your vehicle will be here when you need it, Nicole. Sound good?"

"That sounds like a great plan to me. Are you okay with taking Gwen to Deborah's, Reese?"

"That's no problem," he said.

"You okay with that, Deborah?" Gwen leaned over and asked. Deborah smiled up at her friend and nodded. "Okay, then, if you're ready, Reese, let's head out of here."

Reese grabbed the cane next to him and stood. After receiving promises from Nicole to call and let him know how Abby was doing, he bent down so Deborah could give him a hug. Gwen gave Nicole a quick hug too and tossed a wave behind her as they walked out.

Nicole let out a long sigh as she leaned back into the chair. Deborah saw the toll finally take its effect on Nicole as exhaustion settled across her body. Looking across the room, Deborah got the attention of a nurse who was scurrying through the waiting area.

"Could we have a ... blanket please?" she asked as she motioned to Nicole, who was almost out in the chair.

The nurse glanced at Nicole, smiled, and gave Deborah a quick nod. A few minutes later, the nurse reappeared with a couple of heated blankets draped over her arm. She laid one over Nicole, who pulled it up under her chin; then she turned and wrapped the other around Deborah. Deborah accepted the blanket with thanks and then settled back for news on Abby.

"Nicole ... Nicole," Deborah said as she gently nudged Nicole.

"What ..." Nicole stammered as she tried to come out of a fog of restless sleep. It took her a minute as she tried to get her bearings, but as soon as she saw Abby's doctor heading across the busy room, she woke right up. A blanket that was tucked around her fell to the floor as Nicole stood. She wondered for a split second where the blanket had come from but quickly tossed the thought aside as the doctor came to stand in front of her and Deborah.

He gave them a reassuring smile as he said, "Abby is doing fine and is the proud owner of a purple cast."

"Can we see her?" Nicole asked.

"She is on her way up to 4West as we speak. That's the pediatric wing, and a room was made available, so we sent her on up there. The nurse at the counter can tell you how to get up there, or someone can escort you if you want."

"We have a friend coming back with an overnight bag for me and to take Deborah back home. How will she find us?"

"That's no problem. Just make sure the nurse knows, and she will give your friend directions to where you are when she gets here."

Nicole and Deborah thanked the doctor for all his help as he walked away. Nicole turned and walked behind Deborah's wheelchair so she could push it over to the nurses' counter. She stopped as she leaned over to unlock the brakes of the wheelchair and paused a minute.

She put her hand on Deborah's shoulder and said, "Thanks for staying with me. I really did need someone to hold vigil with me. I'm glad it was you."

Deborah reached up and gently squeezed Nicole's hand, too moved to reply. Nicole unlocked the wheels and pushed the wheelchair over to the nurses' station. After getting directions and leaving Gwen's name, they headed for the elevator that would deliver them to Abby's floor. A few minutes later, they were escorted into the room where her sweet baby lay. Nicole was surprised to find that Abby was awake, though still a little groggy.

"Mommy," her small voice creaked.

Nicole went over to her daughter and gave her a big smile. "How's my sweet baby girl?"

"I want to go home," Abby said, fear creeping into her voice.

"Shhh ... you're fine. Mommy's here, and I'm not leaving."

Deborah rolled closer to the bed and laid her hand on top of Abby's good arm.

"Gramma?" Abby said with a slur.

"Yes, sweetie ... it's Grandma. Everything is going ... to be okay. You just shut your eyes ... and rest."

Within minutes, Abby was asleep. Nicole leaned over and gave Abby a gentle kiss on her forehead; then she stood and stared down at her daughter for a few minutes more before stepping back. Deborah did not release her hand from Abby's arm as she continued to stare at the child asleep peacefully next to her. She only pulled her eyes away when she heard Nicole sink into the recliner on the other side of the bed. Compassion filled her as she looked into the tired eyes across from her.

"Nicole, when ... did you eat?"

"I don't remember."

"Go and eat. I'll stay here."

Nicole was shaking her head. "Can't eat, can't leave her."

"Then order something. Not doing you or Abby any good ... if you get sick."

"There you guys are," Gwen said as she stood in the doorway with Nicole's overnight bag in one hand. "I see our little girl made it through okay."

"Yes, she was awake when we first came in, but she's out again."

"Nicole needs ... to eat," Deborah stated firmly.

Gwen lifted an eyebrow to Nicole. "Sounds like an order to me. Want me to go to the cafeteria and get you something?"

"No, you don't need to do that. I can order something and have it sent up here."

Gwen looked from Nicole to Deborah and said, "I think I need to get you back home, Deborah. You look like you're about to drop where you are, and Nicole needs some alone time with her daughter."

Deborah looked as though she wanted to protest but took one look over at Nicole and relented. She had to admit that she was feeling the strain too.

"Promise to order ... some food?" she asked softly.

"Promise," Nicole said as she stood and walked around the bed. "And thank you, both of you, for being here. It means so much to me and Abby."

Gwen gave her a quick hug, and Nicole leaned over and gave Deborah a soft kiss on her check.

"We'll call you in the morning and check on you and Abby," Gwen promised.

Nicole nodded and watched as they made their way out of the room and down the long hall to the elevator. She turned back to Abby and gently stroked her daughter's soft cheek. She took a breath and settled into the recliner next to her daughter's bed. A sense of *déjà vu* hit her as she remembered doing the same thing not so long ago in Deborah's hospital room. A deep sigh left her as she pulled a blanket up over her lap and sank down into the chair for the night.

Chapter 17

"**M**ommy."

At the sound of Abby's tiny voice, Nicole rose from the recliner where she had spent a restless night watching over her daughter. The recliner was more functional than it was comfortable, and Nicole's senses were on hyperdrive. She had heard every breath Abby breathed, every movement her precious child made, and every time the machine beeped or a nurse came in to check on Abby.

"I'm right here, sweetie," she said as she stood next to the bed. She leaned over and offered a smile as she took Abby's hand in her own and rubbed it gently with her thumb. "Mommy's been here all night, watching over you."

"You my angel?" Abby asked.

Nicole smiled again as she said, "Yes, I'm your angel."

"I got a purple one," Abby declared as she raised her cast up to show Nicole.

"Yes, I know. I wonder how they knew purple was your favorite color?" Nicole teased as she ruffled Abby's thin, blond mop of hair.

Abby giggled and said, "You told them!"

Nicole leaned over and gave her daughter an Eskimo kiss, which sent Abby into even more giggles.

"What is all the noise coming out of this room?"

Nicole looked up to see the day nurse step through the door. The name on her badge said Lucy, and Nicole remembered her from the day before. Lucy was a big lady in height and girth but had shown such gentleness with her patients that Nicole knew the stern voice was just a façade.

As did Abby, who started laughing as she reached her good arm up and pointed at Lucy. "You're not willy mad!"

Lucy smiled as she made her way across the room. "You got me. Besides, how could I be mad at such a sweetie like you? It's just not possible. I was just jealous that you were in here having all the fun!"

"Would it be okay for me to order her breakfast?" Nicole asked as she watched Lucy go through her routine of checking Abby's vitals.

Lucy put her stethoscope in her ears, leaned over, and listened quietly to Abby's chest. After listening a few seconds, she stood back up and looped the stethoscope around her neck. Turning to Nicole, she smiled and said, "I don't see any reason to starve this young lady. I can order it for you if you'd like."

"Thanks, that would be great. She loves oatmeal."

"With brown sugar," Abby added.

"Oatmeal with brown sugar. Do you want juice with that, young lady?"

Abby smiled as she nodded her head in agreement. Lucy turned and headed for the door. She paused before leaving and added, "How about you, Mom? Would you like anything?"

"Coffee would be wonderful," Nicole said with a sigh.

"You got it. Take anything in it?"

"Got any flavored creamer?"

Lucy threw her a smile as she opened the door and said, "I think we can hook you up with some Carmel Delight."

"Yes, that would be great. Thank you."

"No worries. I'll be back soon with that."

"One more thing," Nicole interjected. "When will we be seeing her doctor?"

Lucy glanced at her wristwatch and said, "He should be here anytime, actually. Dr. Phillips usually does his rounds first thing in the morning."

"Okay, thanks," Nicole said. She turned back to her daughter and leaned her arms on the bedrail as she said, "Do you know what people get to do with your cast?"

Abby looked up at Nicole with large, saucer-shaped eyes and shook her head no.

"Well, young lady, they get to get sign it! What do you think about that?"

"Really?" Abby asked with a serious face.

"Yes, really," Nicole replied, "and I would like to be the first one to sign it."

Abby's face burst into a smile as she quickly nodded her head and held her cast up for Nicole to sign.

"Let me get a marker out of my purse." Nicole stood and grabbed her oversized bag from the recliner in the corner. Long ago, she had learned to always be prepared for anything. It worked well with being a nurse and a mom to a special needs child.

She rummaged through her bag and finally lifted a red fine-point marker triumphantly out of it. A few minutes later, she had inscribed, "Love you forever and ever, Mom" in flowing letters on the top of Abby's cast with the *o* in the shape of a flower. Abby was admiring her mom's handiwork when there was a small tap at the door.

"Gramma! Aunt Gwen!" The small child exclaimed in delight. Nicole looked up to see Deborah filling the doorway in her wheelchair with Gwen standing behind her.

"Come on in, you two," she said as she stood and moved a chair aside so Gwen could push Deborah's chair closer to the bed. Gwen positioned and locked Deborah's chair before leaning over to admire Abby's cast.

"Well, look at you! That's pretty snazzy! Can I sign it too?"

Abby nodded her head excitedly as she held up her cast for Gwen. Nicole handed her the marker, and Gwen signed the cast. Abby read the small get-well message and giggled. "Thanks, Aunt Gwen. Gramma, you sign?"

Nicole took one look at Deborah's face and said, "Why don't we wait until we get you home? There will be plenty of time to get signatures."

"Have you heard when you can bring her home?" Gwen interjected.

Nicole shook her head. "I'm still waiting for the doctor to stop by."

Deborah reached out and took her hand in her own. "Sure it will be … soon. House too quiet."

Nicole smiled at her as she squeezed her hand. "You may regret those words once we get her home."

"No, don't think so," Deborah responded, and it took her breath away as she realized that she meant it. The house had seemed so empty the past few days with Abby and Nicole both here at the hospital. She started to realize just how much they both had become an important part of her life. Her throat constricted with emotion as she tried to say more but was cut off by a knock at the door.

"I got some oatmeal with brown sugar for our Miss Abby," Lucy announced as she walked over with a tray and set it on the side table next to Abby. She deftly swung the whole thing around so that it was positioned in front of Abby, and after a few minutes of adjusting the bed and pillows, she seemed satisfied that Abby could reach her oatmeal and juice with no problem.

"Just push the call button if you need anything," she said as she strode back out of the room.

"Thanks," Nicole said over her shoulder as she leaned over to tie a bib around Abby's neck.

"Mrs. Brennan."

Nicole turned to greet Dr. Phillips as he strode past Lucy and into the room. She had been expecting him all morning and was anxious to get Abby home and into her own bed.

"Hi," she said as she shook the hand he extended.

"How's our fairy princess doing this morning?" Dr. Phillips asked as he walked over and examined the cast on Abby's arm. Abby raised her round face up at the doctor and giggled in delight at being compared to a princess. "That's some nice artwork you have there. Who's the artist?"

Abby gave him a shy smile and said softly, "Mommy and Aunt Gwen."

Dr. Phillips smiled back at her as he finished his exam and gently tousled her hair with his long fingers. "I'm sure you'll have that filled up in no time."

"Do you think Abby can go home today?" Nicole asked, her hands clasped tightly in front of her. She noticed that Dr. Phillips's smile tightened as he turned back to her, and Nicole's stomach clenched in response. Something wasn't right. She could see it in his eyes.

He looked back at Abby, who had gone back to attacking the oatmeal. "Abby's arm is doing nicely. I don't see any reason that it won't heal with no problem."

Nicole let out a sigh of relief but then noticed that the tension was still in Dr. Phillips's expression. He turned back to Abby. "Is it okay, Abby, if I borrow your mommy for just a minute?"

Gwen looked from the doctor to Nicole and said, "You mean I can have this precious girl all to myself for a few minutes? By all means, take your time. I got a little something for Abby that I think she is going to love."

"What, Aunt Gwen?" Abby asked, her attention completely on Gwen now. Nicole mouthed *thank you* to Gwen as she turned to follow the doctor out of the room. She paused as she started to go around Deborah.

"Is it okay if Deborah comes?" The doctor hesitated for half a second, and Nicole added, "She's Abby's grandma. She's family."

The doctor nodded his head, and Nicole reached down to unlock the wheels. Deborah grabbed her hand as she reached for the handles to turn the wheelchair around. Her eyes said it all as they locked with Nicole's. Nicole smiled down at her and quickly squeezed her shoulder as she pushed the chair and followed Dr. Phillips to a private sitting area at the other end of the hallway.

Dr. Phillips motioned to a chair on one side where Nicole could set Deborah's wheelchair next to her and then pulled a chair over so he was seated directly in front of them. Leaning forward, Dr. Phillips propped his elbows on his knees and spoke softly. "We heard a murmur when we did our initial assessment when we admitted Abby yesterday."

"Murmur?" Nicole asked, her mind racing, trying to understand what he was saying.

"Yes, I ordered an echocardiogram …"

"Her heart!" Nicole cried out and reached for Deborah's hand.

"Abby has an opening between the left and right sides of her heart," Dr. Phillips continued. "All babies have it before they are born, and normally, the hole seals itself up at birth. Occasionally, it does not seal itself off like it should, and that is the case with Abby."

"How serious … is it?" Deborah asked, her voice shaking.

"It needs to be taken care of, the sooner the better. I already spoke with Dr. Jennings at the Children's Hospital here in town. He's the best pediatric cardiologist in the state. He can take Abby and do the procedure tomorrow morning."

"You're talking about invasive surgery," Nicole said. She felt the blood draining out of her face just imagining it.

"Yes, but it's a very common procedure. Kind of like a heart cath. Dr. Jennings has done hundreds of these procedures," Dr. Phillips said, trying to reassure Nicole and Deborah. "Abby couldn't be in better hands."

"I'm sure he is, it's just … heart surgery," Nicole exclaimed, her face ashen.

"I know, it sounds scary, but it really does need to be taken care of before it gets worse."

Deborah squeezed Nicole's hand. "Abby is strong … like her mother."

Nicole looked over at Deborah then nodded. "Okay, I guess we should do this."

Dr. Phillips nodded his agreement at the decision. "I've already got all the paperwork going for her transfer over there. All we need is for you to sign the consent form."

Nicole felt her body go numb as she nodded her consent. Dr. Phillips squeezed her hand as he stood up to leave. "Dr. Jennings will go over the details of the actual procedure when you get there. I'll have your nurse get you those release papers to sign."

He stood and paused before leaving. "If you have any other questions or need anything, just have the nurse get hold of me."

Nicole just stared into space, too numb to respond. Deborah squeezed her hand and thanked the doctor as he strode away. She put her hands on Nicole's face and gently pulled her around so that she could look her in the eyes.

"It is going to be fine," Deborah said in a slow, firm voice, her eyes penetrating Nicole's with strength. "God's got her. He will take care of our precious child."

Nicole looked into Deborah's eyes and nodded as she let the tears come. Deborah hushed her softly as she drew her into her arms and let her cry.

Chapter 18

A few minutes later, they were back in Abby's room. They had stopped by the nurse's station on the way back so Nicole could sign the release papers that Lucy had ready for her. Now she had to find a way to explain to her daughter that she wasn't going home but to another hospital. How could she possibly explain this to her daughter when she didn't understand it herself?

"I'm all done, Mommy!" Abby proclaimed as they came into the room.

Nicole tried to plaster as bright a smile as she could onto her face as she locked the wheels on Deborah's chair and walked over to stand next to her daughter. She grabbed a cleaning tissue from a pop-up container on the end table and gently wiped away as much of the mess around her daughter's mouth as she could. Abby's face scrunched up as she tried to pull away from her.

"There, I knew you were under that mess somewhere."

"Look what Aunt Gwen got me!" Abby exclaimed, pointing at a stack of coloring books and assorted crayons and markers on the table next to her food tray.

"I see," Nicole acknowledged as she leaned over and gave Abby a soft kiss on her forehead. "I hope you thanked Aunt Gwen for getting them for you. That was very nice of her."

Abby nodded her head as Gwen spoke up. "She most certainly did, and it was my pleasure."

Nicole glanced at Gwen and Deborah and then turned her attention back to Abby. This was not going to be easy to tell her daughter, but she was glad she had Gwen and Deborah there for support.

Abby's large, almond-shaped eyes looked up at Nicole as she asked, "What wrong, Mommy?"

Nicole sat next to her daughter and put her arm around her as she said, "The doctor was just explaining to your grandma and me that he would like to send you to another hospital, a special hospital, that can help you get better."

Abby's expression was confused as she looked up at her mom and said, "I want to come home, Mommy. I don't want to go to 'nother hospital." Her lower lip started to quiver as tears pooled in her eyes, and Nicole pulled Abby close to her to hide her own tears.

"We want you to come home too, sweetie, but the doctors found something that they need to fix first. So they're going to take you to a special hospital that can take care of this little problem and get you back to us as soon as possible."

"Do I get to ride in an ambulance?" Abby asked.

Nicole nodded, and Abby smiled for a second at the thought but then turned serious again. "Will you come with me in the ambulance?"

"I don't think so, sweetie—there won't be enough room. But I'll be there when you get there. I promise."

Abby looked from Nicole to Deborah to Gwen and back to Nicole. "Don't worry, Mommy. I'll be okay."

"Oh, I know you'll be okay because I know who is watching over you."

Abby smiled and said, "Jesus!"

Nicole swallowed her up in her arms and hugged her as tight as she could.

"You are my best blessing," she whispered in Abby's ear. She held her daughter out at arm's length so she could look in her almond-shaped eyes. "I love you so much I can't breathe."

Abby smiled up at her mother and then threw her arms around her neck. "I lub you to the moon and back."

Nicole smiled at the familiar words that they had shared ever since Abby could speak and squeezed her daughter even harder.

"Well, are you two going to hog all the hugs and love going on in here, or can a couple old ladies get in on this lovefest?" Gwen asked, standing on the other side of the hospital bed with her hands plastered on her hips. She wore a scowl on her face, but it did not mask the smile that was bubbling its way to the top.

"I second ... that motion," Deborah stated next to Nicole and then surprised everyone by pulling herself up using the handrail on the other side of Abby's bed. Making sure Deborah was steady enough, Gwen stepped back as Deborah used the rail to sidestep to the head of the bed. Once Deborah was standing at Abby's side, her friend stepped back next to her and put her hand on the small of Deborah's back to help steady her.

"Come here ... precious," Deborah said as she leaned forward, reaching out her good arm toward Abby. Abby quickly filled the space between them and gave her grandma a tight embrace. "Grandma loves you so very much."

"I love you too, Gramma."

"Okay, that's it," Gwen proclaimed as she reached over to engulf both Abby and Deborah in a hug. "I need to be part of this lovefest!"

"Woo! Didn't know I would be interrupting a group hug!"

Nicole turned around, still chuckling from the theatrics going on in front of her, and exclaimed, "Michael! It's so nice to see you again!"

"Mickey Mouse!" Abby screeched from the bed as she unwrapped herself from Deborah and Gwen and reached her arms out to the nurse who had helped her in ER. Michael strode over to the bed and leaned over for his hug.

"Mickey Mouse?" Nicole asked with a raised brow.

"Yeah, it seems to help with little ones if I use my nickname, which is Mickey," Michael said as he pulled himself up. "Of course, some of them latch onto referring to me as Mickey Mouse, like this one!"

Abby giggled and tried to turn her head away before he could grab her nose, but Michael was too fast for her. "There, I got it! Now what are you going to do?" he said, pretending he had her nose in his hands.

"Give it back!" she said, giggling as she reached her hand up trying to reach his. Michael appeared to be contemplating whether to give Abby her nose back or not; then he sighed and put his fist back on her nose.

"Okay, you win, young lady."

"You must have heard," Nicole said, "they're sending Abby to Children's Hospital."

"I did hear something about that," Michael said as he turned back to Abby. "As a matter of fact, they so happen to need a nurse to go with them, and I volunteered!"

"Really?" Nicole exclaimed, relief washing over her. Abby wouldn't be nearly as scared in the ambulance, and she was sure Michael would make it an adventure for her little girl.

"What do you think, Abby?" he asked, turning back to the young patient propped up in the bed. "You think you'd like me to come with you? Because if not, I'm sure I could find Wile E. Coyote to go."

"No! Not Wiley! You!" Abby could hardly contain her excitement.

Michael chuckled and turned back to Nicole with his arms outstretched. "Guess I'm going then."

"Thank you, Michael. You have no idea how much this means to all of us."

Michael pushed her gratitude aside with his hands. "No worries. She's something special. I didn't have to think twice about it."

He turned and gave Abby a quick wave goodbye and left to get everything set for the ambulance ride. Nicole felt as though a huge weight had been lifted off her shoulders. Gwen came around to give Nicole a hug. When she let go, Nicole looked over at Deborah, who still stood by Abby. She let go of Gwen and walked over to Deborah.

Tears choked her as she pulled her former mother-in-law into her arms and held onto her.

"God ... is so good," Deborah whispered.

Nicole stepped back and saw the same tears in Deborah's eyes that she had been holding back in her own, and she stopped trying and let them come.

"Yes, He is," she said.

"Has anyone thought to let Reese know?" Gwen asked, stepping up behind Nicole.

"No," Nicole conceded, wiping her eyes with the back of her hand. "I did get hold of Kathee to let her know, but with getting the transfer ready and everything ..." Nicole stopped and looked at Gwen and Deborah with a shrug. "Sorry, I guess I'm a bit overwhelmed. Here, Deborah, let's get you back to your chair first. Then I'll text Reese and let him know what is going on with Abby."

Deborah didn't resist Nicole and Gwen as they helped her get back to her chair and made sure she was safe and comfortable. As soon as Deborah was situated, Nicole pulled out her phone and scrolled down to Reese's name. She wrote him a quick message explaining as much as she could what was happening and that they were on their way to Children's Hospital and sent it over to him.

"There, it's sent," Nicole said as she powered her phone down and put it back in her purse. "I'll give him a call when we get over there and settled. Now I guess we wait. I'm sure Lucy will have some idea on when we can expect to be leaving."

Nicole turned tired eyes to Gwen and Deborah. She could see the concern reflected back in both of their eyes. Letting out a sigh, she said, "It's been a busy morning. Gwen, why don't you take Deborah back home? There's nothing either of you can do here. You and she can both get some rest."

Deborah started to protest, but Nicole just held her hand up to silence her before she could say anything. "I know you want to be there, Deborah, but trust me, this is a long process. It will probably be late afternoon before we even get over there. You go home with Gwen now, get some rest, and come up tonight to see Abby after she is settled in her new room."

Nicole looked over at Gwen. "You okay with staying with Deborah? If you can't, I got a name of an agency that can come and help."

"Don't even worry about it. I got this," Gwen said as she shooed her away with a sweep of her hands. "You got enough on your plate. You just worry about that precious little girl over there, and I'll take care of Deborah."

"Thanks," Nicole said. She gave both women a long hug as they left the room. Lucy squeezed by them with a smile.

"Well, young lady," she said as she sauntered over to the closet and opened the door, "looks like someone is going on a trip. I'm here to get you all packed and ready."

The next few hours flew by as Lucy scurried around getting everything all set. Before Nicole knew it, Michael and another attendant were at Abby's door with a gurney to take her to the waiting ambulance. Nicole watched as they transferred her daughter from the hospital bed to the gurney. As soon as they had all her belongings tucked away under the gurney, they paused for mother and daughter to have a quick goodbye.

Nicole had to swallow a lump in her throat as she gave Abby a quick kiss and promised that she would see her soon. Then she grabbed her jacket and purse and followed them out into the hallway. She watched as they made their way down to the elevators that would take them back down by ER, where an ambulance was waiting to escort them to Children's Hospital.

As soon as her daughter was in and the elevator shut, Nicole turned and made her way down to the elevator at the other end of the hallway. She got out at the lobby and walked briskly through the front hospital doors to where her car was parked in the long-term patient parking lot.

Chapter 19

Reese shifted uncomfortably in the seat as he sat in the office of Dr. Mary Kinkaid, the army psychologist assigned to assess him. He knew it was just a technicality, another hoop to jump through for the army so he could be discharged to start his new life as a civilian.

A normal life.

Reese had no idea what that meant. His normal was the army, with his comrades he fought side by side with. Those he depended on to keep him safe and who relied on him for the same.

Who would have his back out there, in the real world? he thought sadly.

"Reese."

Shaking the thoughts out of his head, Reese sat up straighter, folding his hands in his lap, and gave the young woman who sat across the desk from him his full attention. Mary Kinkaid was dressed pristinely in her crisp uniform, her blond hair pulled back into a tight bun at the base of her neck. A pair of glasses that framed her blue eyes perched on her small button nose. Reese refocused his attention to what she was saying.

"Everything seems to be in line for you to be discharged. We should be able to get this all wrapped by the first of next week."

Reese nodded his head. He held no false expectations that it would be the first of the week. The gears turned slowly in the service, but he was accustomed to that. What he wasn't used to was waiting. He was and always had been a man of action. That was why he had been drawn to the army and had joined up as soon as he graduated high school. He had planned on making the army his career, his life.

Now, because of his injury, he was being discharged with honor. What was he supposed to do with that? He had no idea. His life, which had once been planned out and clear, was now muddy and unsure.

Mary Kinkaid shut his folder in front of her and leaned forward, her arms resting on her desk as she looked intently at him. He could see the concern in her eyes and looked down at his clasped hands. He had not been comfortable with the gentle probing she had done during their time together. Talking had never been his forte; action was.

"I think there are some issues we still need to talk about."

Reese looked up and matched her gaze. "I don't understand, ma'am."

Mary Kinkaid sighed as she took her glasses off and leaned back in her high-backed leather chair. She rocked there a second as she contemplated him.

Reese shifted uncomfortably as he waited her out.

Finally, she leaned forward with her arms resting on his file. "I don't think you've been completely honest with me, or yourself, about how what happened over there has affected you."

Reese turned cold, dark eyes toward her. He kept all emotion out of his voice as he said, "That's not true, ma'am. I answered all your questions, passed all your required tests."

"How do you sleep, Reese?" she asked as she settled back once more into her chair, watching him intently.

Trying not to squirm under her gaze, he locked eyes with her. "I sleep just fine."

That was a lie. He couldn't remember the last time he had had a good night's sleep. There were too many thoughts going through his head, too many memories ready to jump out of the crevices he had them tucked away in. No way was he going to acknowledge that to the lady in front of him. He was going to answer the questions so that he could get out and start his new life, whatever that was.

"Do you find yourself jumping at loud noises?" she probed.

"Ma'am?"

Mary Kinkaid sighed as she once more leaned toward him. "I think you suffer from PTSD, and I would like to recommend that you continue getting therapy for that. Whether you do that here with me or at another facility doesn't matter. I think it would benefit your assimilation back into civilian life."

Assimilation. He couldn't even fathom what that would look like, but he didn't flinch as he looked back at his therapist. "I'll be okay. I'm going back home to Maine with my family. I'll have all the support I need when I get there."

"Okay, but I am going to strongly recommend that you continue meeting with a therapist when you get home, Reese. I'm sure your family loves you, but they haven't been through what you've been through. They have no real idea what help you need to get through this."

Like having your best buddy die in your arms, Reese thought as his mind went back to that day six months ago. The continuous explosions had had them cornered. They had fought back, trying to keep alive until help reached them. Another battalion was on their way, but it was looking hopeless. The Taliban had them surrounded and were relentless in their onslaught.

He remembered yelling into his SAT phone, asking when they were going to get some relief one minute and being thrown on his side the next, his friend Marc lying across him, as a grenade landed and exploded feet from where he had sat just moments before. He had sat up and pulled Marc and himself around the wall to safety. When they were safely behind the wall, Reese had immediately seen the severity of his friend's injuries. So much blood …

"Reese?"

He shook the images out of his head as he gave his attention back to his therapist and nodded. He had tried to deal with the memories, but if truth were told, the demons were winning.

"Sure, I'll do it," he said quietly.

Mary Kinkaid let out an audible sigh of relief as she pulled a piece of paper in front of her and started scratching on it as she spoke. "That's the best thing you could do, Reese. I'm glad you see that. That's half the battle. I will put you in touch with a therapist I know out there. His name is John Henry."

She raised a hand to Reese's raised eyebrow. "I know, I know, and believe me, so does he, but I wouldn't make any assumptions about the man until you meet him."

"Fair enough," Reese agreed as he leaned back in the cushioned armchair. A smile touched his lips as he tried to envision John Henry and how he had grown up with a name that was sure to have sparked a lot of taunting. A respect for the man filled him.

"I will be in touch with you, then, when everything is settled," the therapist said as she stood and walked around her desk.

Reese reached for his cane, which leaned against the front of the desk. He stood and shook her outstretched hand.

As Reese walked out into the busy hallway, his phone vibrated. He took it out and saw he had a message from Nicole. He quickly read the message Nicole had left and then swore under his breath as he picked up his pace and made his way out to his rental car. He flung himself into the driver's seat, started the engine up, and quickly pulled out of the parking lot.

Reese replayed the message in his head as he wound through the heavy afternoon traffic. His jaw grew tense as he picked up his phone and punched in a number.

"Mrs. Brennan? This is Reese, ma'am. I just got Nicole's message. What happened? I thought Abby was fine." Reese quickly looked in his rearview mirror, switched lanes, and headed for the nearest entrance ramp of the expressway.

Deborah's voice was shaky as she answered him, and he couldn't be sure whether it was from her stroke still or whether she was upset over the newest developments with Abby. He listened as she told him all she knew about what was going on with Abby, but after a minute, it was obvious that she was too upset to go on. Reese waited a second, and then he heard Gwen's voice. She was able to give him some better information about what was going on with Abby, but it didn't do anything to alleviate his concern.

"Where did they take her?" he yelled above the noise of the traffic. "Okay, got it. I'm going to head over there now and check on Nicole. See if she needs anything. Do you need me to come get Deborah? Does she want to be there?"

Reese expertly swerved his car into the right-hand lane and made his way up the entrance ramp. Gwen assured him that they were fine for now.

"Okay, then. If you change your minds, let me know. I'll call you with an update later."

Reese hit the *end* button and tossed the phone in the passenger seat. He gripped the steering wheel with both hands as he picked up speed and raced toward the Children's Hospital downtown. His mind was reeling with all the implications of what was going on, and he shook his head to clear the thoughts. If there was a god, he hoped he was watching over Abby and Nicole right now.

His thoughts went back to conversations he and Marc had had when they were over in Afghanistan. Marc was open about his faith and beliefs, and even though Reese saw that there was something different about Marc, he continually turned away from what Marc was trying to say. His heart was closed to what Marc was telling him, and he didn't want any part of it.

A god that cared, sent his son to die on some cross to what … save us? Reese shook his head as he turned into the parking structure. He grabbed the ticket that spat out of the machine and drove the rental car past the uplifted gate.

Life had taught him that the only person he could depend on was himself. Still, he thought as he pulled into the first parking spot he saw and got out, there were times when he wished he had listened more to what his friend had been saying.

Nicole was pacing the waiting room on the third-floor pediatric cardiac unit when Reese found her. Her eyes filled with tears when she saw him from across the room. Reese strode over to her and ushered her to some chairs in the corner, where they could have some privacy.

"How's Abby?" he asked as soon as they sat.

"Fine, I think," Nicole said as she grabbed a handful of Kleenex off the table and started twisting them with her hands. "I only got to see her for a quick minute when she got off the ambulance. She looked so small and scared."

Reese swallowed hard, trying to imagine what Abby must be going through. He didn't know what to say to Nicole. He had no idea what it was like to have a sick child to worry over, but he knew that Abby had stolen a piece of his heart in the little time he had known her.

"I can't believe you came," Nicole said, interrupting his thoughts.

"Of course I came. I called Deborah to see how she was. Gwen is with her."

"Good," Nicole said as she nodded her head. "Thanks for checking on her. I've been too busy to call myself. I was concerned about her."

"She'll be fine. What about you?" Reese asked, leaning in toward her. "How are you holding up?"

Nicole gave a slight shrug of her shoulders and offered him a wobbly smile. "I'm okay. I'm just worried about Abby. She's all I got in this world."

Reese lifted her chin so she could look in his eyes. "Abby is the most important person in your life, I get that, but she is not the only person in your life. There's Deborah and Gwen and me. We all care about Abby too. We are all here to help you shoulder your pain and concern. That's what friends are for."

"Thanks—I needed to hear that. I guess with all that's been going on with Abby, I'd forgotten that I am not an island. God has surrounded me with lots of love and support. He really has been amazing through all of this."

Reese leaned back, uncomfortable with where this was going. When had Nicole gotten religion? He expected to hear that religious stuff spew out of Marc's mouth, but he hadn't expected Nicole to do the same.

"I'm just waiting for them to get Abby in a room," Nicole was saying. "I talked with the doctors here, and they want to do the surgery first thing tomorrow morning."

"What exactly are they going to do?" Reese asked, his brows furrowed in concern.

Nicole lifted her hands with a slight shrug as she said, "I'm not really sure; they didn't go into any real details. I know she has a hole in her heart, in the wall between the right and left sides. It's something all babies have while they are in the womb, and usually at birth, it seals itself off and the heart starts working like it should. In some children, it doesn't, and they have to go in and seal it up. That's what happened with Abby."

"I don't understand. Wouldn't her doctor have been able to tell?"

"I asked the same question. I guess sometimes the hole is so small it's not as noticeable. Either the accident made it more detectable to hear, or the impact caused it to get larger." Nicole stopped as her voice choked up. She waved away Reese's outreached hand as she tried to get hold of herself. "The doctors say this is a common procedure and not to worry, but … it's my daughter they're talking about."

Reese folded his hands in front of his legs and looked down at the floor. He was at a loss on what to say that would be any comfort to Nicole. Finally, he looked back up at her and said, "I'm not a praying man, Nicole. Not normally. But I was praying all the way here for Abby. I don't have your faith, and I doubt I have much clout, but if praying will help, I'll do it."

Fresh tears filled Nicole's eyes as she reached over and put her hand on Reese's. "Thanks. You have no idea how much that means to me. Your prayers matter, Reese. God hears each and every one of them."

Reese just nodded as the words escaped him. He cleared his throat as he looked over at Nicole. "Is there anything I can do for you?"

A tired smile crossed her lips as she patted his hand before withdrawing it. "No, coming here was so nice of you. It was good to see a face I knew. It grounded me, reminded me that I wasn't alone in this. Thanks for that. I think I would just like to spend a quiet evening with Abby once she gets to her room."

"Okay," Reese said as he stood up. "Will you let me know when they decide to do her surgery?"

"Yes, I will," Nicole said with a nod of her head as she stood also. "Thanks again, Reese, for everything."

Nicole reached up to him and wrapped her arms around his neck. Reese put his arms around her waist and pulled her into a warm hug. She rested her head on his shoulder for a brief second before pulling away. She smiled up at him as she stepped back. Reese nodded his head at her and then turned and walked away before Nicole could see the tears welling up in back of his eyes.

Chapter 20

Nicole sat next to Abby's bed, lightly rubbing her daughter's tiny hand. The surgery had gone without a hitch, and the hole was successfully sealed with a mesh material that the doctors had skillfully sewn in. Nicole was amazed at the technology that made it possible for the procedure to be done with just a couple of tiny incisions. It would help make Abby's recovery much easier and quicker. After a few hours in recovery, Abby was back in her room, still groggy from the surgery.

"Hi," Nicole said softly as she leaned in closer. "How's my little girl feeling?"

"Tirsty," Abby said, licking her dried-out lips.

Nicole reached over for the cup of ice chips on the table next to the bed and scooped a few onto the spoon provided.

"Here you go," she said as she gently placed the spoon on Abby's lips.

Abby opened her mouth and let the ice cubes slide over her tongue. She sighed with contentment as the ice cubes melted and slid down the back of her throat. As soon as they were gone, she opened her mouth for another small scoop, which Nicole had ready for her. After a few more scoops, Nicole set the cup of ice back on the table and took her daughter's hand again.

"Did that help?" Nicole asked. Abby nodded her head as she gave her mother a sad attempt at a smile. Nicole chuckled and leaned over to plant a soft kiss on Abby's head. "That's my brave little girl."

Nicole rubbed noses with her daughter as she pulled her into a hug. She couldn't get over how much she loved this little girl. This past week had made her realize how empty her life would be without Abby, and all she wanted to do now was hold onto her tightly and never let her go.

"Guess what?" Nicole said as she reluctantly released her daughter and let her lie back down into her pillow.

"What?" Abby asked, her eyes looking up at her questioningly.

"You got some visitors who would like to come in and say hi. Think you feel like a little company?"

A smile lit up Abby's face as she nodded her answer. Nicole laughed as she leaned over once more and planted another kiss on her daughter's head. "I'll go tell them that they can come say hi real quick. They've been waiting quite a while."

Nicole left Abby's room and walked down the hall to the family waiting area. She smiled as she remembered turning and seeing Reese standing in the doorway of Abby's room shortly after they had taken Abby in for her surgery. She had felt such relief that he had come to sit with her. Then he had stepped aside, and Nicole had wept to see that he had gone and gotten Deborah and Gwen also. They had sat with her for hours, usually without saying a word, but words had not been needed. Just having them there had been more than she had hoped for.

She stepped into the small waiting area and smiled as they all raised expectant eyes up at her. "Abby is awake and ready for visitors. Would you like to come down and say hi to her real quick?"

Gwen and Deborah both smiled as they nodded enthusiastically, but Nicole noticed that Reese took a step back into the room. "Reese?" she asked, raising an eyebrow at him.

He waved at the two older ladies in front of him and said, "I think you all should have some alone time with her first. I can come in and say hi before we leave."

Nicole nodded and thanked him for being understanding. She went to grab Deborah's wheelchair but stopped as the older lady reached up and grabbed her hand.

"No," she said as Nicole looked at her in surprise. Deborah pointed shaky fingers at the walker over on the side of the room. She had insisted on bringing it, even though Gwen and Reese had used a wheelchair from the front entrance of the hospital to bring her up. "I want to walk."

"Are you sure?" Nicole asked, looking intently into Deborah's eyes. "It's a long hike down the hallway to her room."

"Walk," Deborah insisted again, her eyes and chin set in determination.

"Okay, then," Nicole agreed rather reluctantly.

Gwen grabbed the walker by the wall and set it in front of Deborah. Deborah reached up, grabbed the handles, and with some ease, pulled herself up and stood. She flashed Nicole and Gwen a crooked smile.

Deborah made her way down the hallway with Nicole and Gwen following at a safe distance behind with the wheelchair, ready to step in and offer assistance if needed. Abby's eyes lit up when she saw Deborah come into her room.

"Gramma!" she exclaimed as she sat up in bed, excited.

"You lay right down there," Deborah gently admonished as she pulled herself next to Abby's bed. "If you hurt yourself ... they'll make me leave!"

Abby promptly lay back down into her pillows, but the smile was still all over her face. She could tell that Deborah wasn't really angry with her. Deborah reached over the bedrails and cupped Abby's face with her hand. "Miss you, sweetie."

Abby looked behind Deborah as her mother and Gwen entered the room.

"Aunt Gwen!" she said with outreached arms.

Gwen set the wheelchair aside and went to the side of the bed to give Abby a quick hug. "Oh, we've missed you so, little one. That house is way too empty without you."

"I want to go home," Abby said as a small pout formed on her lower lip.

"Now, now," Deborah said as she pulled Abby's face back toward her. "You have to be a good girl for the nurses and doctors and get well so you can come home. We want you to be all better."

"I think when you do come home, we'll have a party to celebrate," Gwen added. "How would you like that?"

Abby nodded her head as she looked happily from Gwen to Deborah.

"Okay then," Nicole interjected from where she stood at the foot of the bed. "For that to happen, you have to do everything the doctors and nurses say so you can get better and come home soon."

"I will!" Abby promised as she lay back down.

"Good," Nicole said. "Give Grandma and Aunt Gwen a kiss, then. They have been here all morning with Mommy waiting to see you, but they're tired too."

Abby gave each of the older ladies a hug and kiss and waved as Nicole led them out of the room.

"A party? Really?" Nicole whispered as soon as they were out of earshot. "I'm surprised you didn't tell her there would be a clown and pony too."

"Who says there won't be?" Deborah said with a tilted head, but the corners of her mouth quivered as she vainly tried to keep the smile away.

"You two are going to spoil her," Nicole stated as she shook her head. She chuckled softly as they walked back into the waiting area. Reese looked up as they entered.

"What's going on with you ladies?" he asked.

"Nothing, except these two told Abby that they were throwing a party for her when she gets home," Nicole said as she put her hands on her hips.

"What's wrong with a party? I think it sounds like a good idea," Reese said.

Nicole pointed an outstretched finger at him and said, "You're not helping. Do you want to come and say hi before you take these ladies home?"

Reese smiled as he grabbed his cane and walked past her into the hall. Nicole turned back to Gwen and Deborah before following Reese.

"No pony," she warned, pointing a finger at each of them. Feeling she had made her point, Nicole turned and followed Reese down the hall.

Gwen and Deborah quietly looked at each other for a second.

"She didn't say no to the clown," Gwen said with an uplifted eyebrow.

"No, she did not," Deborah said with a wry smile.

"Guess we have a party to plan with a clown," Gwen said with a chuckle as she gave Deborah a high five.

"Well, we have a clown for the party," Gwen said triumphantly as she hung up the phone. "Who would have thought it would be so difficult to rent a clown? Not to mention expensive!"

Deborah looked up from the list she was going over. Both she and Gwen had been hunkered down at her kitchen table all morning trying to get the party finalized, and the clown was the biggest and worst headache of the whole thing.

"I can't believe … there's an actual clown union," Deborah said as she shook her head in disbelief. "But we did it. I cannot wait … to see Abby's face when she comes home Saturday."

Gwen paused as she reached to pour herself another cup of coffee and then finished getting her cup ready. She wrapped both hands around her cup as she rested both elbows on the table and quietly contemplated her friend.

"You know, you referred to here as *home* a couple of times now when we've talked about Abby. I'm just wondering where Nicole fits in all this. They are kind of a package deal, you know."

Deborah set down the pen she had been using and leaned back in her chair. Abby wasn't the only one who had been making progress over the past weeks. It seemed as though Abby's accident and surgery had also lit a flame in Deborah's resolve to improve her situation. She had worked with more determination than ever, and it had paid off.

Not only was the wheelchair a thing of the past, but she hardly used the walker anymore, though they hadn't gotten rid of it entirely. Now she was able to get around quite comfortably with a cane. She realized that she would probably always need a cane, but she was okay with that.

The use of her arm was also improving, and she was now able to use it a little more, though her writing still looked more like a child's; but she kept pushing on, determined it would improve even more. Her speech therapist had been ecstatic at their last session at how far Deborah had come, and a smile touched Deborah's lips at the memory.

"I have been thinking a lot about my life ... since Nicole showed up," Deborah said as she looked over at her friend. "I was so angry at her ... at God ... that I couldn't see what was right in front of me. I blocked everything and everyone out of my life."

Gwen reached over and quietly took her friend's hand.

"It took having a stroke for God to get my attention," Deborah continued. "He had to put me in a place where I had to depend on Nicole, and that was ... so hard. But something happened," Deborah lifted her arm to her chest, "in here. I started to feel ... something. I watched Nicole as she took care of me. Never once did she complain, and I gave her plenty of reason to, trust me."

A flicker of a smile touched Gwen's lips as she patted her friend's hand. "I saw the same thing. Nicole never said one negative word about taking care of you. She didn't do this out of some kind of commitment or obligation. She did this out of love."

"'But the greatest of these is love.'"

"Yes, that was what Christ preached was the number one thing we could do for each other," Gwen said softly.

Deborah looked at her friend through tear-filled eyes. "I have treated her so unjustly. I see the difference in her from before. I see how much she tries." Deborah took a quick breath to choke back the tears. "Gwen," she said softly, "I want to go to church Sunday. I need to go to church. Will you take me?"

Gwen reached over and pulled her friend into a hug. "I would love to," she whispered in Deborah's ear. "I would love to."

"I have another favor," Deborah added as she pulled back from her friend. "I want to go see Gerald Finney."

Gwen raised an eyebrow at the request. "No problem. Can I ask why you need to see your insurance agent?"

Deborah patted her friend's hand as she pulled hers back, a satisfied smile on her lips. "There's something I need to take care of, is all."

"Okay, then," Gwen said. "Let me know when, and I will be sure you get there."

"Thanks, Gwen. You're a good friend. I'll give Gerald a call Monday and see when I can get in there."

Chapter 21

"You two sure outdid yourselves," Nicole said as she checked out the large chocolate sheet cake that spelled out "Welcome Home, Abby!" in purple, Abby's favorite color.

She looked around the family room. There were balloons everywhere! And all the area from the family room to the back patio outside was filled with some kind of activity going on.

There was face painting in one corner of the backyard and a kid whom Nicole recognized from the youth group at church doing magic tricks in the other. Not only were there kids from Abby's school and church, but Nicole was surprised when Kathee showed up too, with her three boys in tow.

And of course, there was the clown.

Nicole just shook her head in amazement and awe at what she saw. Abby was enjoying the whole thing, and it was great seeing her daughter getting to be the center of attention and taking it all in. She still remembered Abby's face when they came in and were both surprised to see what Deborah and Gwen had done for them. It was all so overwhelming.

"You're not mad?" Deborah asked, looking sheepish.

"How could I be mad?" Nicole said as she stepped over and embraced Deborah in a warm hug. "You have no idea how much this means to Abby and me. Thank you."

"It was our pleasure," Deborah said as she patted Nicole's arm.

"Mommy! Look what the clown made me!" Abby was holding up a balloon twisted into a large purple-and-orange flower in her good arm for Nicole to see.

"Wow! That is the prettiest flower I think I have ever seen," Nicole said as she leaned over and pretended to smell it,

"It don't smell, Mommy," Abby said with a giggle. "It's just pretend!"

Nicole acted surprised as Gwen walked up to the three of them. "Hey, Miss Abby. How about I take you out back and you can get your face painted? Would you like that?"

Abby nodded her head and raced off in front of Gwen to where the lady was sitting, doing face painting on Kathee's youngest son. Kathee strolled back inside and took a seat on the couch next to Nicole.

"Abby sure is having a good time, as are my boys. This is really great."

"I'm so glad you and the boys could make it," Nicole said as she squeezed her friend's hand. "This was such a nice surprise."

"Well, I'm glad Gwen and Deborah thought to include us. That was very thoughtful of them."

"It couldn't be a party for Abby without you and the boys," Deborah stated with a small smile.

"Oh, my," Gwen said as she collapsed into a nearby chair. "I had forgotten how much energy kids Abby's age have! I'm way too old to keep up with them!"

"Looks like things are starting to wind down a bit," Kathee said as she started to stand. "How about I get the kids rounded up and get them their cake and ice cream?"

"Sounds like a good idea," Nicole said as she stood to join her friend.

"No," Gwen said as she waved Nicole back into her seat. "Kathee and I got this."

"You won't hear me complain," Nicole said as she sat back down.

"Good," Gwen said. "You've had a lot on your plate lately. Kick back and relax for a bit."

"Thanks, you two."

Both Gwen and Kathee smiled as they made their way to the kitchen.

An hour later, the party had wound down. Everyone had gone, including the clown, the other helpers, and most of the children. Abby, along with Kathee's boys, had crashed out in the living room, and Nicole felt like she could do the same.

"You look beat," Kathee said as she stuffed paper plates of uneaten cake into a large trash bag.

"I'm fine," Nicole said as she filled another trash bag with the same from another table. She paused a minute as she watched Gwen and Deborah cleaning up around the patio. "I can't believe they did this for us. It's a little overwhelming. I feel so blessed, Kathee, I really do."

"I know," Kathee agreed as she came to stand by her friend. "You got some good friends there."

"Who'da thunk?" Nicole said with a smile as she looked at her friend.

"Yes," Kathee said with a chuckle as she gave Nicole a quick squeeze before going back to their cleanup. "It's too bad Reese couldn't make it," Kathee said with a sidelong look at her friend.

Nicole shrugged as she wiped down the table. "Gwen said he had rehab this afternoon. He was real sorry to miss it but said he would stop by early next week to see Abby." Nicole gave her friend a quick hug as she walked past her. "I'm glad you're staying over tonight. It'll be nice to have some time with you before you guys leave to go back tomorrow."

"It was nice of Deborah to offer to have us stay."

"Yes, it was," Nicole agreed. She took her overfilled trash bag to the garage door and set it outside. "I think we're about done. Why don't we go see if we can help Gwen and Deborah finish up out there so we can all put our feet up?"

"Sounds like a plan," Kathee said in agreement as she opened the door leading out to the garage and tossed her trash bag outside next to Nicole's.

"Hey, you two," Nicole said as she pushed open the sliding door and stepped out onto the patio. "Need any help finishing up out here?"

"No, I think we're just about done here," Gwen said as she held the bag open for Deborah, who stuffed the last of the streamers into the already overflowing trash bag.

"Here, let me take that," Kathee offered as she reached for the bag out of Gwen's hands.

"No, I got this," Gwen said as she secured the top and tossed the bag to the side with the rest of the pile.

"Have a seat, girls," Deborah said, motioning to the patio table. "It's been a long day. We're all beat. Nicole, would you mind grabbing the last of the iced tea out of the fridge? I made it earlier."

"Sure, no problem," Nicole said. She went back into the house and returned a few minutes later with the pitcher of iced tea and glasses for everyone.

"Thanks again, you two," Nicole said after she took a sip of her tea. "This was amazing."

"It was no problem," Gwen answered, waving the comment off with her hand. "You know we love that sweet child. This was a small gesture on our part."

"Really?" Nicole said with an uplifted eyebrow. "If this is a *small* gesture, I'd hate to see what a *grand* gesture would look like."

The ladies chuckled at that and then fell into a comfortable silence as they drank the tea and relaxed from the day's events. After a few minutes, Deborah looked around the table and cleared her throat as she set her glass down. "I was wondering if you would like to join us for church before you leave tomorrow, Kathee."

Both Nicole and Kathee looked up in surprise. Nicole found her voice first. "Church? What have I missed?"

"I decided that it was time for me to go back to church. Abby's scare has made me think a lot about getting back."

"That's wonderful," Nicole said quietly as she reached for Deborah's hand. "I'm so happy to hear that."

"And I would love to go with you in the morning," Kathee added, joining her hand with theirs.

"Great—that's settled, then," Gwen said as she stood and began to gather their glasses and the pitcher of tea. "It's been a busy day. I suggest we all get a good night's sleep. I'll pick Deborah, and whoever else will fit in my car, up in the morning. The rest can follow me there."

"Sounds like a plan," Nicole said as she smiled over at Deborah.

"Ugh!" Kathee said as she threw her head back. "We got to get those kids upstairs and into bed. You know how hard it is going to be to wake them up after the day they've had."

"How about we just throw blankets on them and we sleep in the recliners down there?" Nicole suggested. Kathee gave her a doubtful look, to which Nicole shrugged. "I've slept in worse these past few weeks. Trust me."

Kathee laughed as she stood to join her. "You have a point. I guess it would be easier."

"It'll be fun!" Nicole said as she put her arm around her friend and guided her inside. "We can stay up and talk all night. It will be like camping, sort of."

The only response she got back from Kathee was a *harrumph*. Nicole threw back her head and laughed as they made their way inside.

Chapter 22

Reese could hear laughter as he walked up to the front door of Deborah's Cape Cod. He paused a moment before pressing the doorbell. He had thought about Nicole a lot over the past week since last seeing her. Last night, he had made a decision.

Nicole deserved to know the truth. It wasn't his place to judge her or withhold information he knew about Marc. Besides, the past few weeks with Nicole had showed him how much she loved her daughter and how well she took care of Deborah, even though Reese was pretty sure it had been a difficult road for her to go down.

What had surprised him the most, though, was how open she was about her faith. Marc had always been up-front with Reese about his own faith, but Reese had always assumed that Marc was a better person than him, and it seemed natural that he would have a god that would love him. Reese didn't feel like he fell in that same category as Marc and had just blown Marc off.

But seeing that same faith in Nicole had made Reese rethink everything he thought he knew. Could what Marc had told him about

God and forgiveness and unconditional love all be true? Could God really love him too? Reese shook the thoughts aside as he pressed the doorbell button and took a step back. He smiled as Abby ran up to the door and pushed it open with a giggle.

"Uncle Reese!" she yelled, throwing her short, chunky arms around his good leg.

"Abby! Be careful! You almost knocked Uncle Reese over!" Nicole exclaimed as she came up behind her daughter. She looked apologetically at Reese. "Sorry about that. She gets a little excited."

"No worries," Reese said as he gently patted the top of Abby's head. Abby lifted her face and looked adoringly up at him. He quickly gulped down emotion that suddenly caught him off guard. Abby released her hold on his leg as she grabbed his hand with her good arm and started tugging him into the house.

"We built a fort!" she exclaimed as she continued to pull him down the hall to the family room. "Come see!"

Reese could hear Nicole chuckle behind him as they made their way to the back of the house. "Sorry, but she's pretty excited about this. We've been working all morning on this fort."

Reese came to an abrupt stop as they turned into the family room and just stared. The family room had been converted into a giant tent city. The whole room was now covered with blankets and quilts and sheets.

"Wow," was his only response as he continued to stare.

"Come look, Uncle Reese!" Abby exclaimed as she ran into the middle of the mayhem and disappeared under a blanket in a far corner. A few minutes later, she poked her head out of a quilt draped over the sofa and coffee table. "You want to come play?" she asked innocently.

Reese glanced down at his cane, and regret filled him that he couldn't do what Abby asked of him. Nicole noticed his discomfort and stepped in.

"Abby, Reese just got here. Why don't you play with your dolls you got under there for a bit? Grandma and Aunt Gwen will be home soon, and you can show them too. Okay?" Abby smiled as she nodded her head and dove back under the covered furniture.

"Thanks," Reese said.

Nicole waved her hand in dismissal as she headed over to the breakfast table. "Abby will forget all about us. She's got all her American Girl dolls and every stuffed animal imaginable under there. She'll be fine for hours."

"Gwen and Deborah are out?" Reese asked as he sat down. He leaned his cane on the chair next to him and stretched his leg out in front of him. It had a tendency to stiffen up on him otherwise.

"Yes," Nicole said as she started to sit down and then thought better of it. "I just made a fresh pot of coffee," she said over her shoulder as she made her way back to the kitchen. "Can I get you a cup?"

"That would be nice. Thanks," Reese replied.

Nicole poured coffee into two large mugs and brought them over to the table. She set Reese's in front of him as she sat down next to him, still holding hers in her hand. She wrapped both hands around hers and inhaled deeply. A smile of contentment touched her lips as she leaned back into her chair.

"Do you think they will be back soon?" Reese asked, trying to sound nonchalant, but the question caused Nicole to lift an eyebrow at him.

"Not really sure. Deborah was pretty tight-lipped about where they were going when Gwen picked her up this morning. She didn't hesitate at all when I asked if it would be okay if Abby and I made a fort back here. Though I don't think she was expecting it to be such a massive undertaking when she said yes. I know I didn't, but we had so much fun doing it. I hope Deborah won't regret saying yes when she sees it."

Nicole glanced at the clock on the kitchen wall. "It is getting late, though. I expect they should be home anytime. I can't imagine what she had to do that would take her this long."

Reese nodded his head distractedly as he picked up his mug and took a sip. "This is good," he said as he set it back down.

"What is it?" Nicole asked, leaning forward, her arms resting on the table as she stared intently at him. Reese could tell that she wasn't fooled. She could tell he had something gnawing away at him. "Tell me."

Reese shifted uncomfortably in his chair and threw a glance at where Abby played. He had really hoped Deborah would be here too, though he didn't really know why. A part of him felt she needed to hear what he had to say too, but then, maybe he should tell Nicole first, but not with Abby around. This really needed to be done in private. He wished he had thought it through a little bit better. He cleared his throat and started to think of an excuse to leave when he heard the front door open.

"That must be Deborah and Gwen," Nicole said as she threw him a curious look.

A few minutes later, both women walked into the room and came to a stop. Reese watched Nicole's face as she tried to gauge Deborah's response to what she and Abby had done to her family room.

"I'm sorry, Deborah," she apologized. "We kind of got carried away this morning when we were doing it. Abby wanted to keep adding on, and before I knew it, it had taken over the whole room."

"Gramma!" Abby yelled as she popped out from underneath the blankets. "Come look at my tent!"

Deborah laughed as she walked carefully over to where Abby was, taking it all in as she went. "This is really nice!" she exclaimed as she gave Abby a big hug. "You did a very good job, sweetie!"

"Wow," Gwen said as she came over to sit with Reese and Nicole. "Looks like Aladdin paid a visit. I have to say I'm impressed."

"Thanks," Nicole said. "I wasn't sure how Deborah would respond when she saw it."

"Oh, I think she is full of surprises," Gwen said coyly. Nicole glanced over at her, her eyebrows knitted together at the remark, but Gwen ignored her as she glanced at their cups. "Great! You made coffee!" She jumped up and went to pour herself a cup.

Deborah made her way back to them and sat wearily in a chair next to Nicole. "Pour me one too, Gwen."

"You guys were gone all morning," Nicole said as she took another sip.

"Looks like we made it home just in time," Deborah quipped with a smile. "Might have taken over the kitchen and dining table too if we had been any longer."

"Yeah, I'm sorry about all this. I'll have it all picked up tonight after Abby goes to bed."

"You and Abby worked hard to put this together, and she's having fun. Leave it up for a few days."

Gwen walked back over and handed Deborah's cup to her. Deborah wrapped her hands around the warm cup and rested it in her lap as she pulled her attention from the tent city to Reese.

"Good to see you, Reese. I was hoping you would stop by for a visit."

Reese fidgeted in his seat as he looked down at his hands for a second. Then he turned his eyes back up to look at the group of women in front of him and said softly, "I stopped by because there's something I need to tell Nicole. It's about Marc … and the letter she sent him."

Nicole took a quick intake of breath, shock registering on her face as the words registered. "Marc got my letter?" she said in barely a whisper. Tears formed in the corners of her eyes, and she leaned forward, her hands shaking as she wrapped her fingers tighter around her mug.

Gwen looked from Reese to Nicole, stood, and cleared her throat. "Abby," she called. The little girl popped her head out of where she was at, all smiles. "You want to go for a ride with Aunt Gwen? We can get some ice cream."

"Okay!" Abby said. A minute later, she had made her way to the exit closest to Gwen.

"Deborah?" Gwen asked, giving her friend the nudge to leave also. Deborah started to stand, but Nicole put her hand on her arm to stop her.

"I would like Deborah to hear this too," she said as she looked intently over to Reese.

Reese nodded his head in silent agreement. Deborah looked down at Nicole, her eyes full of questions. Nicole met her questions with a small nod and tugged her arm to pull her back down. Nicole's hand slid down Deborah's arm and found her hand. She grabbed Deborah's hand and wrapped her fingers tightly with the older woman's.

Gwen told Nicole to give her a call when they were ready for her to bring Abby back. She smiled down at Abby, who was dancing excitedly at her feet.

"Yeah, just what you need—more sugar," she said with a sigh. A few minutes later, the front door shut, and they were gone. Silence surrounded the small group for a moment.

"Please, go on," Nicole prompted. "You said Marc got my letter?"

"Yes," Reese said as he leaned forward, resting both elbows on the table. "Marc got your letter, Nicole. About a week before ... before he died."

A small gasp came out of both women at his words. Nicole turned tear-filled eyes to him and asked, "What did he say? Did he tell you?"

"Marc was overcome with joy, Nicole. Honestly, I didn't understand it." Reese looked at Nicole apologetically. "I saw how devastated Marc was when you left him. He was a mess."

Nicole looked down at the floor, fresh shame filling her over her own actions so long ago. Reese leaned in closer and pulled her eyes back to his.

"Marc forgave you, Nicole. He explained that if Christ could forgive him, a sinner, then he in turn could forgive you. I honestly thought Marc was crazy. I didn't understand."

Nicole's shoulders sagged as she started to sob uncontrollably. Deborah released her hand and put her arm around Nicole's shoulder, pulling her gently to her. Tears glistened in Deborah's eyes as she looked back at Reese.

"Please continue," she said.

"Marc could talk of nothing else but that letter. He carried it with him in his front pocket and was always pulling it out to read. He told me that he was so excited because you had accepted Christ too. He said that he had been praying a long time for you." Reese paused a moment before going on. "He told me a lot of things that were on his heart that last week. He wanted to see if there was a chance for the two of you ... and Abby ... to become a family."

Nicole's head snapped up. "He said that?" she asked incredulously. "Marc wanted to give me, us, another chance ... after everything?"

Reese nodded his head slowly, letting what he had said filter through Nicole's head and settle into her heart. Nicole looked shell-shocked, and Reese couldn't blame her. It was news that she had never expected, he was sure. Deborah, her own eyes watery, continued to draw her close, giving Nicole strength and support as best she could.

Nicole turned her tear-filled eyes toward the older woman, and unspoken words vibrated through them. For the first time, Reese noticed closeness between the two women that he had not seen before. Whatever doubts he had had about sharing this information were gone.

"The only thing that Marc loved more was the picture of you and Abby," Reese said as he continued with his story. "I swear, he acted like he was a new daddy. Anyone could tell that he loved her as though she were his own."

A fresh sob rumbled up Nicole's throat as she put her hand up to hold it back. The pain was so raw that she couldn't hold it in. "He loved ... my little girl," she sobbed. "I don't deserve his love. I don't deserve it."

"Shhh," Deborah whispered as she pulled Nicole closer. "That last week of Marc's life was the happiest for him. Your letter ... gave him joy and hope ... and God made sure it reached him in time before He took him home."

Reese dropped his eyes to the floor, feeling like an intruder on such a private moment. He didn't say anything as the two women held onto each other and rocked back and forth in their shared joy and grief. Finally, Nicole pulled herself away and sat up, wiping the tears away with the backs of her hands.

"I cannot thank you enough, Reese," Nicole said softly. "There are no words for the gift you have given me and Deborah."

Reese hesitated a second as he reached into the pocket of his jacket, which lay next to him on the arm of the chair. Gently, he pulled out a long envelope and looked at it as he continued. "The day after Marc died, I was asked to go through his personal things and get them packed up to send back home to his family. In it, I found this envelope." Marc paused and raised his eyes to look at Nicole. "It was addressed to you."

Nicole drew in a deep breath as she stared at the envelope in Reese's hands. Reese extended the envelope out to her. Nicole's hands shook as she took the envelope that was addressed to her in Marc's strong handwriting from Reese.

Deborah cleared her throat and started to stand. "I think Nicole needs to be alone right now." She looked down at Nicole with a sad smile, patting her shoulder. "You take all the time you need. We'll be here when you are done."

Nicole sat in her chair for a minute, frozen, lost in her own thoughts. Finally, she stood and looked at Deborah and Reese. "I need to read this someplace where I can be alone."

Deborah nodded her understanding. "Will you be okay, or do you want one of us to be with you?"

"No." Nicole spoke softly. "I want to do this … I need to do this … alone."

"Okay," Deborah said and watched helplessly as Nicole grabbed her jacket and left.

Chapter 23

Nicole stood silently in front of the gray marble headstone, a gentle breeze blowing her hair into her face. She pushed her hair back and tucked it behind her ear as she sat down on the green patch in front of his name.

Marcus James Brennan
Beloved Son & Brother

"I'm so sorry you're gone, Marc, but I'm also sorry that you couldn't also have 'beloved husband and father' listed, because you were a wonderful husband, better than I deserved, and you would have made a great dad."

Nicole dropped her head and sobbed as fresh regret washed over her. Memories of her life with Marc replayed through her head as she remembered all they had had and all that she had given up. Her shoulders shook as she let the tears pour, unleashing all the anguish and guilt she had held in since hearing of Marc's death.

Now, to hear that he had gotten her letter and had forgiven her was more than she could bear. One question kept digging at her.

How could Marc have forgiven her when she could not forgive herself?

Nicole knelt in front of the headstone. Leaning forward, she lightly brushed her fingers over the top of Marc's name.

"I miss you," she said softly. "I wish you could have gotten to know Abby. Heard her sweet laugh and silly giggle. Picked her up in your strong arms and held her tightly. But mostly, I wish we could have had a life together, and I am so sorry that we didn't, even if it had to be so very brief. I don't know how I will ever be able to move past that."

A soft breeze nudged her, and off in the distance, Nicole heard a cardinal chirping. She took in a deep breath and felt a calmness overtake her, and she knew that she wasn't alone. She had someone watching over her, and He had been there since the day she had accepted Him as her savior. He would be there for her always.

Nicole slipped her hand into her jacket pocket and pulled out the envelope Reese had given her. With shaky fingers, she slit open the top and took out the handwritten piece of paper. She took in a deep breath as she slowly unfolded it and began to read.

Dearest Nicole,

I received your letter today, and I don't have words to express the joy I felt when I read your news. Ever since we separated, I have been praying for you, that the Lord would work in your life and that you would come to find Him. Everyone around me thought I was crazy when I started jumping up and down after reading that you had found the Lord.

I adore the picture you included of your sweet girl. Abby is such a beautiful name, and she is such a beautiful girl, just like her mommy. She has your smile! I like that you named her after your grandma Abigail. That is so cool. I look forward to meeting Abby one day and holding her in my arms.

I would hope that you know that I have already forgiven you. I did that a long time ago. It's one of Christ's commandments, you know, to forgive and to love one another. I never stopped loving you, Nicole, and I hope when I get back from deployment we can get to know each other again. I would love to be a daddy to your little girl. I love her already.

Until I get to see you, please hold your daughter tight in your arms and keep your eyes on the Lord, and I will hold both of you in my thoughts and prayers too.

Love always,
Marc

Nicole clasped the letter to her chest as she rocked back and forth, tears streaming unrestrained down her checks. Mixed with the sadness was a joy that not only had Marc still loved her, but he had also loved Abby from the moment he had seen her picture. She leaned forward until her forehead touched the headstone above Marc's name.

"I love you too, Marc," she whispered. "I will tell her what a special, incredible man her daddy was."

Nicole paused as she swallowed back tears that threatened to choke her. In a shaky voice, she said hoarsely, "I feel so lost right now, Marc. Where do I go from here, without you by my side?" Immediately, a peace surrounded her, and she knew the answer. The answer that had been there all the time: she was never alone.

She bowed her head and said a quiet prayer of thanks to the one who loved her unconditionally and had promised to never leave her. She held that promise close as tears slid unbidden down her checks.

Standing, she took one last glance at the headstone and gently patted the top of the dark granite. As she turned to walk away, Nicole was startled to find Reese standing a few rows away. He looked down at his feet, clearly uncomfortable at interrupting such a private moment. Nicole quickly wiped the tears away with her hand and walked toward him.

"I'm sorry. I didn't know you would be here," Reese said as he looked shyly at her. "I never would have interrupted you if I had known this is where you were coming."

"It's okay, Reese. Really," Nicole assured him with a small smile.

"I just left Deborah. Gwen and Abby had come back, so she's not alone."

"Good," Nicole said with a deep sigh. Deborah had to be dealing with so much too. It was a lot for all of them to absorb. It hit Nicole that if Reese hadn't come looking for her, then he had come for some time with Marc too.

"I'll give you your privacy," she said as she started to walk away, but Reese reached out with his hand to stop her.

"I came to tell Marc goodbye," he said softly.

Nicole looked up at him, her brow pinched together as realization hit her. "You're leaving?"

Reese nodded his head as he looked away. Nicole could see he was battling with his own feelings and reached out to touch his arm.

"I already told Deborah and Gwen," he said. "I was planning on telling you too, but I wanted to come see Marc."

"What are you going to do?"

Reese blew out a breath and then looked back at Nicole. "Good question. I don't have all the answers yet myself. Guess for right now I'll go back home to Maine and work with my father. He has a construction company that he's always wanted me to be in. It's just that now …" Nicole followed Reese's gaze down to his bad leg, and she understood his dilemma. He would be limited in what he could do on a construction site.

"Well, maybe you just have to find a new avenue," she suggested as she pushed her hair out of her face. "The world is out there, Reese. You're not limited to that small box you have yourself in."

"Yeah, I know," Reese said as he shifted his cane to his other hand. "It's just a lot to chew on when you think that you have your life all planned out. My dad has been looking forward to putting 'and son' on his sign since I was born. It's more his box than mine."

Nicole reached forward and touched his arm, drawing his eyes back to her. "There is a verse I learned when I first came to know the Lord. It says something like "'I know the plans I have for you,' declares the Lord, "plans to prosper you and not to harm you, plans to give you hope and a future.'"

Reese didn't say anything as he pulled himself away. Nicole dropped her hand from his arm and looked back toward Marc's headstone.

"Did Marc ever tell you how we met?" she asked softly. Reese shook his head no.

Nicole nodded and continued as her eyes once more found their way back to the headstone. "I was working at the VA hospital in San Diego as an aide. One day, Marc came in to visit a friend of his who had been injured. His friend had lost his leg while on deployment and was doing rehab there. Marc was there every day, encouraging him, praying with him, and helping him with his rehab. I remember thinking what a special guy he had to be that he would do that for a friend. One day, about a month later, he stopped at the nurses' station where I was sitting and asked me out. I couldn't believe that he had even noticed me.

"We fell in love and eloped six weeks later. Next thing I knew, Marc got orders and we moved cross country over here. It wasn't so bad; we had his family then. Two years later, he got transfer orders to Aberdeen, Massachusetts. Six months after that, he left for deployment." Tears trickled down Nicole's cheeks as she turned and looked over her shoulder at Reese. "You pretty much know what happened after that. My life took a nosedive, and I took Marc down with me."

"Nicole," Reese said as he stepped toward her, but Nicole shook her head at him.

"I'm not looking for your sympathy, Reese. I did what I did, and it is what it is. I can tell you that I had no idea where my life was going before I had Abby. My life was a mess. I was alone and pregnant and lost. I never dreamed I would become a nurse, but having Abby and meeting Kathee opened that door for me. I believe with all my heart that it was the Lord working in my life, even then. He can do the same for you, Reese."

Reese took his arm away and stepped back. Turning from Nicole, he walked over to stand in front of Marc's headstone. Nicole didn't move as she gave him the space he needed. After a minute of silence, Reese spoke without turning back to her.

"I never really considered that I needed God, you know. My mom died when I was young, and it was just my dad and me and my sister, Maggie, for as long as I can remember. We never went to church that I can recall. It wasn't until I met Marc that I even heard about God." Reese shrugged his shoulders as he touched the headstone. "I didn't really think Marc's God could be my God too." Reese paused and brought his eyes back to Nicole. "Not until I met you and saw how it had changed your life."

"Oh, Reese," Nicole said, tears brimming as she took a step toward him. "Jesus came for all of us. None of us deserves the sacrifice He gave for us. He gave his life for each and every one of us. Including you."

Reese swallowed hard as he spoke. "I'm beginning to understand what Marc was trying to tell me. I'm still trying to wrap my head around it. It's a lot to take in."

"When are you leaving, Reese?" Nicole asked.

"Should be anytime."

"I can't believe this is goodbye," Nicole said softly as she came to stand next to him. "Do you think you'll still be here Sunday?"

"I don't know," Reese said with a shrug. "It all depends on if they are finished with my paperwork by then. Why?"

"I would love to have you come to church with us," she said softly, letting the words drift in the wind. "Maybe it could help answer some questions you might have. Besides, we all want to see you one more time."

"I can't promise anything," Reese said hesitantly as he shifted his eyes from Marc's headstone back to Nicole, "but I'll try."

"I hope so, Reese," Nicole said as she reached up and gently touched his cheek with her hand before turning and walking away.

As she walked, she threw up a fervent prayer that the Lord would continue to work in Reese's heart.

Chapter 24

Deborah found herself walking over to the front window again. She had worn a path from the couch to the window since Nicole had left hours earlier. Once again, she leaned on her cane with one hand while the other hand pulled aside the heavy drapes so she could peer out to see if the car she had heard drive by was Nicole. She let the drapes fall back with a sigh when she realized again that it wasn't Nicole pulling into the driveway.

"Deborah, come sit down," Gwen coaxed as she patted the seat next to her. "Nicole will be fine. She just needs time to sort this all out."

Gwen had returned after Deborah had called to tell her that Nicole had left to read Marc's letter alone. She and Abby had stopped and bought Kentucky Fried Chicken for dinner, along with a side of mashed potatoes and corn bread. The three of them had eaten silently; then Gwen had given Abby a bath and tucked her away in bed for the night.

Deborah turned and made her way back to sit next to her friend. She shook her head as she sat down and said, "I never should have let her leave, Gwen. Not alone."

Gwen leaned over and covered her friend's hand with her own. "You can't do this to yourself, Deborah. Nicole is a grown woman. She will get through this. Just give her some time."

"I need to talk with her. There is something she needs to hear, and I need to say it." Deborah looked at her friend, tears glistening in her eyes. "Something I should have said long ago but that I was too full of hatred and anger to see. It left such bitterness in me that I turned away from everything and everyone that matter."

Sobs erupted from Deborah as she turned her face away. Gwen leaned over and wrapped her arm around her friend. Gently, she pulled Deborah toward her and let her friend cry softly on her shoulder.

After a few minutes, Deborah sat up and brushed the back of her hand across her eyes. Gwen grabbed a fistful of Kleenex from the end table behind her and offered them to her friend. Deborah took them and wiped her face dry. She turned to her friend with regret still resident in her eyes.

"I need to apologize to you," she said in a shaky voice. "You are my best friend, and I shut you out. I treated you so badly, and I know it had to have hurt you. I am so sorry, Gwen. Can you forgive me?"

Gwen pulled her back into a strong hug and said, "You silly girl, of course I forgive you. What kind of best friend do you think I am? I never gave up on you. You were always in my prayers. I knew you had to work through all your pain, and even though you wouldn't let me or anyone else close to you help, I knew the Great Healer could. And He has."

"Yes. He has," Deborah sniffed. "He did it by bringing Nicole to me."

"God is good," Gwen said with a soft squeeze. "He knew what you needed, even if you didn't."

"I'm so ashamed at how I treated her, Gwen. I've got to make it right."

"Just tell her what's on your heart."

"I plan on it. If she ever comes home."

"She will," Gwen assured as she threw a quick glance out the window. Dusk had started to fall, and concern filled her.

Please keep her safe, Lord, she prayed.

Deborah sat up straighter and said, "There is something else on my mind. Something I've been thinking about for a while. Since this all happened."

"What?" Gwen asked.

"I think it's time I put this house up for sale," she said slowly.

"Really?" Gwen said in surprise.

"Yes," Deborah said, her head nodding in resolve as she continued. "This place is too big for just me, and with all the bedrooms upstairs, it isn't practical. I do need to get the outside painted."

"Todd Johnson from church is good, I hear."

"Good," Deborah said with a nod. "I'll give him a call tomorrow."

"Where would you go?"

"There's a new senior living complex going up, not too far from our church."

"Yes, I've seen it going up. It looks very nice."

Deborah nodded her head and continued, "I would like to go and check it out. Maybe fill out an application if I like what I see."

"I can take you anytime," Gwen said with a smile.

"Thank you," Deborah said as she squeezed her friend's hand in gratitude. Her thoughts turned back to Nicole, and she threw up another prayer just as headlights turned into the driveway.

"Looks like Nicole is home," Gwen said with a sigh of relief as she stood. "I am going to head out. You two need some time alone, I think."

Gwen grabbed her coat and slung it over her arm. Pulling her purse up over her shoulder, she reached over and gave her friend a quick hug.

"I'll be praying," she said softly into Deborah's ear. She made it to the front door just as Nicole was walking in. Giving her a quick hug, Gwen said she would see her later and that Abby was safely tucked in bed for the night.

"Thanks," Nicole said as she set her purse on the table by the door and shrugged her jacket off. "I'll check on her in a bit."

Gwen waved at them as she quickly left. Nicole turned and

walked into the living room, where Deborah sat on the edge of the sofa, waiting for her.

"Are you okay?" Deborah asked.

Nicole shrugged her shoulders and said, "I don't know. This is a lot to take in. Not sure I've processed it all yet."

"Well, if you have a moment, would you come in and sit down? There is something I need to say."

"I'm really tired. It's been a long day," Nicole said as she raked her fingers through her hair. "Can this wait?"

"No, it can't." Nicole looked at Deborah with surprise. Deborah patted the couch next to her and said, "Please."

Nicole's shoulders slouched forward with exhaustion, both mental and physical. A part of her desperately wanted to run to her room, get in bed, pull the covers up over her head, and forget the world for a day or two. She had nothing left to give, but there was something in Deborah's eyes. Deborah looked up at her with such pleading that Nicole couldn't turn her back on her. Wearily, she made her way into the living room and sat on the edge of the sofa next to Deborah, silently waiting for the older woman to speak.

Deborah leaned toward Nicole, her voice soft and shaky. "Nicole, can you forgive me?"

Nicole's head snapped up in surprise. She opened her mouth to speak, but the words were lost by tears that threatened to choke her. In a split second, Nicole was off the sofa and kneeling in front of Deborah. Taking the older woman's weathered, age-spotted hands in her own, Nicole spoke hoarsely through her own tears. "What do you need forgiveness for? You've done nothing wrong."

"No, but I have," Deborah insisted. "I refused to forgive you. The one thing God asks us to do. I see now that I was wrong, so very wrong in how I treated you, Nicole."

"Have you forgiven me, Deborah?" Nicole asked slowly, her eyes searching the older woman's.

Deborah pulled a hand out from under Nicole's and gently

stroked Nicole's cheek. "Yes, I forgive you, Nicole. Will you forgive me too?"

Tears streamed freely down Nicole's face as Deborah's words sank in. She felt a closeness and love for the woman in front of her that threatened to overflow.

"You don't need to ask for my forgiveness, Deborah. You've treated me like a daughter from the moment Marc brought me here to meet you. You were never anything but kind and loving to me. After what I did to Marc and your family, you had every right to resent me. I don't hold that against you."

Deborah gripped Nicole's hand tighter as her eyes implored her and said, "I became a bitter woman after I lost Lee and Marc. I let hatred fester in my heart against God and you that hurt me more than anyone else. It kept me from God's grace and love, and most of all, it kept me from seeing what a blessing you were in my life. I let my anger cloud my eyes and my heart, and I am so, so sorry. I have so much regret about how I treated you, Nicole. I've already made my heart right with God. Now, I need to make it right with you."

Nicole pulled Deborah into a tight embrace before she had finished and held her tight. Silently, they rocked back and forth as both ladies let the words heal.

"Yes, I forgive you," she whispered into Deborah's ear.

"From now on ... you are ... my daughter," Deborah whispered back.

Nicole held her tighter, overwhelmed at what Deborah had said. After a few seconds, she pulled back and looked Deborah in the eyes. What she saw reflected back at her were eyes full of love. Love for her.

"I would be so honored to be called your daughter."

Deborah smiled as she took her hands and cupped the younger woman's cheek and said, "I know it's been a long day for you, but would you be interested in a cup of coffee? We have so much to talk about."

"I would love that," Nicole said. "All of a sudden, I'm not tired at all."

Deborah laughed as she reached for her cane. "Somehow, I doubt that, but come along. I got a special blend of roasted hazelnut for a special occasion. This definitely qualifies."

Nicole stood and wrapped her arm around Deborah as they made their way to the kitchen side by side.

Nicole was enjoying the solitude of the garden. Gwen had picked Deborah up first thing that morning to run some errands, and Abby's bus had just picked her up for school. She had just started back a week ago, and Nicole's nerves were finally starting to settle down. She kept repeating God's promises over and over when she felt a panic attack start to come on, but this morning as she watched the bus pull away, Nicole had felt nothing but peace.

Nicole reflected on the night before. She and Deborah had sat at the breakfast table and spoken all evening of Marc and their shared faith over a cup of coffee. Nicole was still a little in shock at what had transpired but knew it all came back to the amazing God they worshiped and loved.

When Gwen showed up, Nicole could tell by the way she looked at the two of them that she knew something had changed. Nicole felt it too. There was a warmth between her and Deborah that had never been present before. She had come out to the garden after Gwen and Deborah had left with her Bible and a glass of iced tea. She had spent some time praying and reading from the Psalms before picking up the phone and calling the one person she wanted to share the news with.

"Hello, you!" Kathee said after only one ring.

Laughing, Nicole leaned back into the chaise and said, "What, were you sitting by the phone?"

"I just got back from the gym and was headed up for a shower before my shift starts. I just happened to be taking my phone out of my jacket pocket when it rang. Glad it was you. You've been on my mind. How are things going?"

"Well, you might want to sit down a minute. I got some news to share that is going to surprise you. I'm still trying to wrap my head around it."

"Good news, I hope?"

"Yes." Nicole took a second to take in a deep breath. "Kathee, Deborah has forgiven me."

There was silence on the other end. Nicole sat up in the chaise, concerned that her friend did not seem to share in her joy. Just as she was getting ready to ask her friend if she was still there, Kathee came on with a loud cheer that nearly burst Nicole's eardrum. Nicole joined in with a mixture of laughter and tears as she recounted last evening's events.

After she was done, Kathee said, "Wow, Nicole. We've been praying for her for so long, and to see God work through you in her life is amazing."

"I can't take any of the credit for this. As you like to say, 'it's a God thing.'"

"That is so true," her friend agreed.

"There's more," Nicole said as she settled back in the chaise. Slowly, she recounted her conversation with Reese at Marc's gravesite.

"That's amazing," Kathee said when Nicole finished. "Do you think he'll take you up on your invitation?"

"I'm not sure. I guess we'll have to wait and see and continue to pray for him."

"I will keep him in my prayers—you know that."

"Yes, I do," Nicole said with a soft smile. "Thanks."

"What are you going to do now?" Kathee asked.

Nicole let out a sigh as she thought a moment before speaking. "I've been thinking about that all morning, actually. Deborah is doing much better. She really won't need me to take of her much longer, the way she's going."

"Maybe it's time for you and Abby to start making a life for yourselves finally," her friend gently suggested.

Nicole let out a long sigh as she laid her head back on the chaise. "You know, it's been such a whirlwind these past four years. First nursing school and then taking care of Deborah—I really haven't had time to think about what is next for us."

"Well, you don't have to make a decision this minute. Abby has another month before the end of the school year. Pray about it and see where God leads you."

"Even if it's back to your apartment above the garage?" Nicole asked with a smile.

She heard Kathee laugh at her end as she said, "It will always be here if you need it. You know that, right?"

"Yes, I do, and I want you to know that I have appreciated all that you have done for me." Nicole stopped as she choked on the words. Her voice quivered as she continued, "You are my best friend. I really can't even imagine where I would be now if you hadn't stepped into my hospital room that day."

"Stop it," Kathee said, tears in her voice. "I love you like a sister. There is nothing I wouldn't do for you."

"I know, but I think it's time for Abby and me to make a life for ourselves. I will pray about it."

"I will pray too."

"Thanks, I know you will," Nicole said softly and hung up. She looked at the garden around her and felt peace settle on her heart. She knew that whatever was in front of her, she wasn't alone. She raised her face to the warm sky, sent a silent prayer of thanksgiving, and asked for direction in her life as she made decisions for the next phase of her and Abby's life.

Chapter 25

Nicole and Deborah slid into the pew next to Gwen, who smiled at them. People had already started to stand as the praise team led everyone in the first song.

Gwen leaned over and whispered in Nicole's ear over the music. "I was beginning to wonder if you all were going to make it."

"Abby had a wardrobe malfunction. Her zipper broke on her jeans, and we had to quickly change," Nicole whispered back.

Gwen chuckled, and they both turned their attention back to the song. Nicole closed her eyes as she lifted her voice up and let the words flow through her. She found that she enjoyed this part of the service as much as she did the message.

Gwen leaned in again as the song ended and asked, "Any word from Reese?"

"No, I was hoping he would show up today, but ..." Her words got lost as the next song started, and she just shrugged her shoulders. Gwen put her arm around her and gave her a gentle squeeze in response.

The song ended, and the praise leader encouraged everyone to greet one another. Nicole turned around to shake hands with a young couple behind her when her eyes fell on Reese standing in the back of the sanctuary. He looked nervous and uncomfortable as he scanned the large auditorium looking for them.

Nicole patted Deborah's shoulder so she could squeeze by her and go to him just as Reese spotted her and made his way down the aisle. When Deborah looked up at her with a quizzical expression, Nicole pointed to Reese, who had slid in the end of the pew and stood next to Deborah. A warm greeting filled Deborah's face as she smiled up at him and lightly tapped Reese's arm in acknowledgement. Gwen reached across Nicole and Deborah to squeeze his arm too. Nicole could see Reese relax as she added a smile of encouragement.

The next song started, and Nicole raised her voice in thanksgiving to the Lord for answering her prayer and bringing Reese to come sit beside them today. Now she prayed that Reese would continue to open his heart to what the Lord was speaking to him.

Reese didn't know what had possessed him to come here. It certainly hadn't been his intention when Nicole had invited him earlier in the week. He had tried to tuck away all the questions that had invaded his thoughts the past week, but they wouldn't go away.

This morning, he had woken up and found himself drawn to see what it was all about. He had gotten dressed in a pair of khaki slacks and a blue short-sleeved button-down shirt and driven to the church Nicole had spoken about. He had hesitated just a moment in his car and almost talked himself into driving away.

What had he been thinking? He didn't own a Bible and wasn't even sure if he was dressed appropriately. He had never been inside a church, and he was sure everyone would know it when he walked in. If he could just slide in a back pew and slide out quietly when it was done, he would be happy.

Of course, Reese knew he couldn't do that. Opening his door, Reese stepped out and made his way across the large parking lot into the expansive foyer. He was greeted by an elderly gentleman who smiled and shook his hand as he welcomed him and then held the door to the sanctuary open for him.

Reese nervously scanned the auditorium looking for Nicole and Deborah, but it was a large auditorium, and he was starting to rethink his decision. He was on the verge of doing a quick retreat out the doors he had just come in when his eyes caught Nicole's. Any secret hope that there would be no room for him next to them was dashed as he saw an open spot on the end next to Deborah. He was thankful that they were toward the back of the large auditorium, at least, and not up front.

Both Deborah and Gwen greeted him with genuine joy and excitement, but Nicole greeted him with a small smile that let him know that she knew how hard it had been for him to come. He felt a relief that she understood and felt himself relax.

His attention was turned to the front of the auditorium, where the praise team was starting another song. Reese followed the words as they were flashed on the large screen but was not familiar with any of the songs. Instead, he found himself watching those around him as they lifted their voices up in worship. He glanced next to him and watched Nicole as she sang with her eyes shut and face uplifted in joy and praise.

The song finished, and everyone was told to sit down. The praise team set down their instruments and quietly walked off the stage as a man Reese judged to be in his fifties made his way up to the stage. The man, whom Reese assumed was the pastor, grabbed a small podium from off the side and set it in the middle of the stage. He leaned his hands on the top and peered out into the sanctuary.

"Have you ever been confused with everything that is happening around you? To you?" the pastor asked, his gaze gently falling over the silent auditorium. "Life just doesn't seem fair at times, does it?"

Reese shifted his weight in the pew as he watched the pastor walk to the side of the podium and lean against it.

"Life is hard. There's no denying it," the pastor continued. "Sometimes, our problems seem more than what we think we can handle. But as believers, we know that we do not have to handle our burdens alone. Our Lord is there to help us carry that burden, but he wants to do more than that, friends. He wants to carry it for us. All we have to do is ask."

Reese leaned forward as the pastor went back behind the podium and opened up the Bible he had brought with him when he went on the stage. He asked the congregation to open their Bibles to a passage in 1 Peter 5.

"Beginning in verse 7", he said as he read aloud in a firm voice.

"'Casting all your anxieties on Him, because He cares for you. Be sober-minded; be watchful. Your adversary the devil prowls around like a roaring lion, seeking someone to devour. Resist him, firm in your faith, knowing that the same kinds of suffering are being experienced by your brotherhood throughout the world. And after you have suffered a little while, the God of all grace, who has called you to His eternal glory in Christ, will Himself restore, confirm, strengthen, and establish you.'

"That's our promise, friends," the pastor said, looking up. "He will always be there. We do not have to go through it alone. I don't know about you, but I hang onto that promise. It's gotten me through some dark days."

Reese lowered his eyes as he listened to the pastor talk. His mind went back to Marc and similar words he had said. It seemed that no matter how tough it got, Marc was never overwhelmed. He always had a peace about him. Reese felt that same peace here, and he didn't understand. What made these people different? Was it as simple as what the pastor and Marc said? It was about putting his faith in a man who lived over two thousand years ago? A man who professed to be the Son of God?

Slowly, as Reese listened to the message, he found himself understanding what the pastor was saying, what Marc had told him. Tears started welling up in his eyes as the pastor ended his message. The praise team had made their way back up front and had softly started playing. The pastor leaned forward and spoke gently into the mike.

"Friends, if you are sitting out there today and you do not know Jesus as your personal Savior, I invite you to come up front while the praise group leads us in our closing song. I would love the chance to talk to you about Christ and show you the way to Him." The pastor straightened and looked out over the auditorium as he continued, "If anyone needs to come to the altar today for any reason, I invite you to come and pray right here. Give your worries and cares to him. Everyone, please stand as we sing."

Reese found his legs were shaking as he stood. He watched as people went forward and kneeled by the steps to pray, and he felt a tug at his heart. He felt a calmness that he didn't understand, and before he had a chance to think about what he was doing, he stepped out into the aisle and made his way to the front of the auditorium to join the others who were already there.

Nicole took a deep intake of breath when she saw Reese step out and make his way forward. It took a moment before the realization hit her of what was happening and tears of joy and thanksgiving washed over her. She felt like she should go stand with him. To let him know he wasn't alone. As she was struggling with what to do, she felt Deborah's hand on her arm and looked over at the older woman.

Deborah patted her arm as she whispered, "I'm going forward … for Reese … and for me."

Nicole started to offer to go with her, but Deborah had turned and started her way to the front already. A peace came over Nicole, and she knew that the Lord would take care of both of them. He didn't need her assistance. She felt Gwen's arm come around her and squeeze her tight. She looked up into her friend's glistening eyes and smiled. Together, they lifted their hearts and voices up to the one who was in charge.

Reese was still overwhelmed by the events of that morning. Walking forward had taken him by surprise. He really didn't remember making the conscious decision to go forward or the walk down the aisle. It had been another force leading him to make that decision. He was even more surprised to feel a hand touch his shoulder a few minutes later and to see Deborah kneeling next to him, praying.

A sense of relief and calmness filled him at having Marc's mom next to him as he made the biggest decision of his life. The pastor came over and knelt with them and helped Reese find the words to ask the Lord to be a part of his life, to give himself over to Him completely. When they were done praying, Reese felt a peace that he had never felt before.

He turned to Deborah and helped her up as they stood. Deborah pulled Reese into a warm hug as she whispered in his ear, "I truly believe that Marc is smiling down on us in heaven right now."

Reese choked back tears as he closed his eyes and returned the hug. After a few minutes, they both felt composed enough to walk to the back of the near-empty auditorium and join Nicole and Gwen, who had waited quietly for them. Nicole and Gwen gave each of them a long hug.

"Where's Abby?" Deborah asked as they started to walk out of the sanctuary.

"Lisa offered to take Abby home with her. Her daughter has wanted Abby to come over for some time. She thought we might need some time to talk." Nicole squeezed Reese's hand as she said, "How about it? You want to come over for dinner?"

"I would love to," Reese said.

A few minutes later, they were each in their cars and had a mini caravan headed to Deborah's.

Nicole hung everyone's coats up and quickly straightened the kitchen as she shooed Deborah and Reese into the family room. Gwen had texted her that she was stopping to pick dinner up on the way over. Nicole found that she had a lot of nervous energy flowing through her, and she needed an outlet for it right now. The memory of Reese going forward that morning was still racing through her mind, and she couldn't slow down her excitement.

Deborah had shared with her on the drive home that Reese had accepted the Lord, and Nicole still marveled at the news. She paused as she wiped down the sink and lifted her eyes up and sent another prayer of thanks. Draping the dishcloth over the sink's center divide, Nicole turned and made her way to join Reese and Deborah.

Reese had pulled the side chair over by Deborah and was leaning forward as the two of them spoke softly together. Nicole cleared her throat as she sat on the edge of the couch across from them. She hated to interrupt their talk, but she also wanted to hear all that had taken place that morning.

Reese looked up with an apologetic smile as he said, "Sorry, I didn't mean to be rude. I just had questions, and Deborah was just explaining some things to me."

"You don't have to apologize," Nicole said with a wave of her hand. "I had a lot of questions too when I first got saved. I was lucky. The Lord put Kathee in my life to help me in my spiritual growth. Deborah is a good person too."

Deborah's face turned red, and she looked uncomfortable. "I wish that were true," she said. "Unfortunately, that has not been the case for a while. Part of the reason I went forward was for Reese, but the other reason was for me. I needed to ask the Lord for forgiveness for rejecting Him this past year."

She turned and clasped Reese's hand in her own. "You see," she continued, "the Lord was speaking to my heart too. I was trying to get up the courage to go forward when I saw you step out. Seeing you take that step forward that we had all been praying for, how could I not?"

Nicole left her seat and kneeled next to the older woman. "You have been through more than any person could endure. Your history of love for the Lord outshines that. You have nothing to be ashamed of."

Tears welled up in the both of their eyes as Nicole reached up and wrapped Deborah in a warm embrace. They were still wrapped in a tight hug when they heard the front door open and Gwen's loud voice announcing that she had dinner from KFC if anyone was hungry. She was telling them about the Sunday afternoon congestion in the KFC drive-through as she entered the kitchen and came to dead stop.

Nicole pulled herself away and started to stand, but Gwen waved her away. "I got this. You just have a seat, and I'll bring the meal to you. I got four of their famous chicken sandwiches with all the trimmings. Figured it would work for everyone."

"That's sounds good," Nicole said as she joined Gwen at the counter. "Let me help."

"It smells good," Deborah added. "My mouth is watering."

Gwen grabbed two plates that she had transferred the sandwiches onto, along with a pickle spear and a side of red-skinned potato salad. She walked over and handed one to Deborah and the other to Reese.

"Thanks," Reese said as he rescued his fork before it hit the carpet. He looked up at Gwen with a grin at the near-mishap and chuckled. "That was a close one."

"You're lucky," Gwen said with a wink. "Deborah would have you doing dish detail for a month."

Deborah looked up and feigned outrage. "Really, I am not the monster she portrays me as. I would only have made you do dishes for two weeks."

Nicole joined in the laughter as she brought drinks in for everyone. Then she and Gwen sat down on the couch with their own sandwiches.

"So Reese, I just want to say how happy we all are that you made a decision for the Lord," Gwen said as she set her sandwich down. "It's a very important decision that is going to impact your life forever. Can I ask what your plans are now? Are you staying around for a little bit? I'm assuming that Pastor John would like to have some time to talk with you, answer any questions you have?"

Reese finished the bite of sandwich he was chewing and set his plate on his knee. He looked at Gwen as he nodded his head and said, "Pastor John did say that he would like to meet with me at least once before I leave."

"When are you leaving?" Nicole asked quietly.

"Tuesday," Reese said. All three women tried to hide their disappointment, but it was hard.

"I'm sorry," Nicole said. "We all knew you would be leaving soon—it's just hard to see you go, especially after what occurred today. This is such a big step, and we are all so overjoyed for you. We just …"

"We just want you to continue to grow," Deborah said, picking up on what Nicole was trying to say. "It's going to be hard for you with no one to help support your new faith."

"However," Gwen said as she looked directly at the young soldier across from her, "you will not be alone. You've got the Holy Spirit in you now, and we will be praying for you. It will be important that you find a good Bible-preaching church. That will be our prayer for you, and that the Lord will bring someone alongside of you to help guide you. The main thing you need to do is read His Word and talk to Him."

"Reese, did you get a Bible?" Deborah asked.

"Pastor John gave me this," Reese said as he pulled out a small New Testament from his shirt pocket. "I'm meeting with him tomorrow afternoon. He asked me to read the gospel of John tonight and said we could discuss any questions I had then."

"That's a good start," Nicole said with a smile.

"Yes. It is," Deborah agreed as she waved Nicole over.

Nicole stood and went over by her. Deborah pointed to the bookcase by the fireplace as she whispered to Nicole. Nicole walked over to the bookcase and retrieved a well-worn Bible off of it. She brought it over to Deborah, who took it and set it gently in her lap. Deborah ran her hand softly over the well-worn cover as she said softly. "This was Marc's Bible. He had it with him overseas."

"I know," Reese said as he folded his hands and leaned toward her. "I saw Marc with it often. He was always reading from it."

Deborah nodded as tears gently slid down her cheek. She looked up at Reese and lifted the Bible and handed it to him. "I think Marc would want you to have this."

Reese couldn't speak as he took the Bible in his hands. He looked at Deborah, and his eyes told her all she needed to know as she reached over and smiled at him. "Never let it leave your heart, Reese. Always treasure the gift you received today."

"Oh my!" Gwen exclaimed as she wiped her hand across her eyes. "I think we need a group hug!"

They all laughed as they kneeled around Reese; then they became silent as Deborah lifted him up in prayer.

Chapter 26

Deborah stared at the phone in front of her. This was a call she was not looking forward to making but knew deep in her heart that she needed to. She had tossed and turned all night thinking about it. It wasn't until she had given it over to the Lord that she had found peace and been able to fall asleep.

Nicole had gone on a field trip with Abby's class to the Pittsburgh Zoo and Aquarium. It was a perfect day for it, and Deborah knew they would have a wonderful time. She and Lee had taken the boys there many times when they were small.

It was also the perfect time to make the call that she had been putting off to Tyler. Taking a deep breath, Deborah lifted the phone off its base and dialed her son's cell phone. She closed her eyes as she listened to it ring at the other end. She was beginning to think that it would go to voice mail and debating whether she should leave a message or not when he answered.

"Hi, Mom. Is everything okay?"

It saddened Deborah that Tyler would think that the only reason she called him was because something was wrong. It was her own fault, she thought. Deborah had come to realize that over the years she had done nothing to strengthen their relationship. No matter how much he had strayed, he was still her son, and she loved him. They were all they had left, and she had to do what she could to fix that.

She tried to keep her voice light as she said, "No, honey, nothing is wrong. As a matter of fact, things are good, real good."

"You sound better," Tyler said, his voice still cautious. "Therapy must be working."

"That has definitely worked," Deborah said. "But it's more than that."

"Yeah? What else?"

Deborah could tell his defenses were up. The last thing she wanted this call to do was push her son further away. The very thought of that happening tore at her heart, but she trusted that no matter what happened today, the Lord would use it to start Tyler's healing and their restoration as a family again.

She took a deep breath before she spoke. "I need to tell you about Nicole."

Silence was the only thing she got from the other end. Thinking maybe the call had gotten dropped, she said, "Tyler?"

"I'm here," Tyler responded tersely. "I've said all I am going to say about her, Mom."

"I know, Tyler, but you don't know what's happened," Deborah interjected. "Tyler, Nicole got a letter from Marc."

Again, there was silence on the other end. This time, Deborah waited for Tyler to speak. Finally, after what felt like forever, he said, "Why would she get a letter from Marc, Mom? They have been over for years. This is just a way for her to get to you. You can't believe what she tells you."

"No, Tyler, you don't understand. After all that happened with her and Marc, she went through a really bad time. She found the Lord through all that, and she has a lot of regret for what she did. She wrote Marc months ago to ask for his forgiveness, and when she didn't hear from him, she came to ask forgiveness from me."

"Mom," Tyler said with a sigh, "I know you have a big heart, but people don't change their true colors."

"No, you're right, Tyler. People can't change on their own; only God can change them. I treated Nicole shamefully when she first showed up on my doorstep. I was so angry at God then that I couldn't find room in my heart to forgive her, but the only person that hurt was me."

Deborah paused for a breath and waited for a response. When there was none, she continued. "Nicole has never showed me anything but respect and love, and trust me, in the beginning, I gave her no reason to stay. No other person would have put up with the treatment I gave her. That was when I started to realize that maybe, just maybe, she had changed. You see, the Lord was using Nicole to open my heart back up to Him too. I had turned my back on Him when I lost your father and Marc. And I realize now that I shut you out too. You were hurting too, and I wasn't there for you. I am so sorry, Tyler. I love you, son."

"I love you too, Mom," Tyler said, his voice softening. "I just don't trust Nicole. I'm sorry, but all I see is the pain she caused Marc and our family. I don't know if I can get past that."

Deborah closed her eyes and she said a small prayer as hope filled her heart. She could hear the uncertainty in Tyler's voice, and she prayed it would be the beginning of healing for him as she said, "A friend of Marc's stopped by to see us. His name is Reese, and he served with Marc. He had a letter that Marc had written to Nicole. You see, Marc had gotten Nicole's letter shortly before … before he died."

Deborah stopped as tears welled up in her throat. Swallowing past them, she continued, "Nicole let me see the letter after she read it. Marc's letter was full of joy and love and forgiveness. He wanted a second chance to build a life with Nicole and Abby. He never got the chance, Tyler, but we do. I already told Nicole that I forgive her and I want her and Abby to be part of my life. I hope you understand and can find it in your heart to do the same."

"I don't know if I can get there, Mom," Tyler said. "I still think she has another agenda." There was a momentary pause before he continued. "I guess if Marc and you can forgive her, I will have to step back. I won't make any more waves, but don't expect me to welcome her with open arms. I don't have your and Marc's ability to forgive like that."

Deborah sent a silent prayer of thankfulness. It was a small step, but it was a beginning, and she knew the Lord didn't need much to change a heart. Smiling, she settled back, and they talked a few minutes about Tyler's job and his recent trip to China. They ended their conversation with a promise to stay in touch more often.

As Deborah hung up the phone, she resolved that as soon as she was able, she would fly out to Colorado and visit with him. It was time they became a family again.

In the meantime, she had things to take care of. The first thing was meeting with the realtor later that morning to put her house on the market. A smile played on her lips as she let that thought settle in. She had no regrets; this had been a good home to raise her boys, but now it was time for her to move on.

A few weeks ago, she and Gwen had stopped by the new senior living project that was going up by their church. After going through their model, Deborah had signed papers for a two-bedroom apartment that would be finished in six to eight weeks.

"Come on, Elijah," she said as she leaned on her cane and stood. The golden retriever looked expectantly up at her from where he lay by her feet. She smiled down at him and said, "It's time for both of us to get moving. We have things to do before the realtor gets here."

Elijah slowly stood and followed lazily behind her into the den Nicole had converted into a room where Deborah could recuperate after her stroke. Deborah reflected about how far she had come since that day, on so many levels. She walked over to the French doors that opened to the back patio and garden.

Taking hold of the door handle, she pulled the door open and stepped out. Taking in a deep breath, Deborah inhaled the many scents that lingered in the air. Smiling, she looked down at the golden retriever, who sat dutifully at her side looking up at her.

"Life is so good, Elijah," she said. "How did I get to be so blessed?"

Elijah's only response was to pant next to her. Deborah laughed as she patted his head and turned to go back into her room.

Chapter 27

Nicole let a smile touch her lips as she hung up the phone. It was the second phone interview she had had this week with a pediatrician's office over by Kathee, and Nicole felt good about it. Kathee was as excited as she was at the prospect of her and Abby moving back and starting their new life. She had even reiterated that they could stay in their old apartment above the garage until Nicole found a more permanent solution.

Nicole chewed on her lower lip as she thought about the move back. She wanted to be excited for her and Abby, but a gnawing thought kept creeping in. Deep down, she realized that she didn't want to leave Deborah. She had grown to love the older woman as family, but Nicole had to face reality. Deborah no longer needed a live-in nurse to take care of her. As hard as it was to accept, it was time for Abby and her to move on.

The real issue was telling Deborah that they would be leaving. She hadn't had the chance to do so yet, but she knew that she couldn't put it off much longer. The past week had been an emotional one, with Reese's salvation and his leaving for Maine almost right after. He had stopped by on his way out of town Tuesday to say goodbye. Abby had insisted that she was going to come spend the summer with him. Nicole smiled at the memory of Reese holding her in his arms as he told her she was welcome anytime. Then he had placed a large cowboy hat on her head and told her she would also need to get some boots when she came.

Nicole heard the front door open and headed toward it. Gwen had taken Deborah out this morning for breakfast and to run some errands. They had been rather vague about their plans, but Nicole had figured it had to do with the move. They had both danced around what would happen when Nicole and Abby moved out.

"Are you two done already?" she asked as she made her way up the hall. "I thought you'd be gone longer."

Deborah was setting her purse and keys on the front table by the door as Nicole got to the front. She was surprised to see Deborah alone and with no bags.

"Where's Gwen? I thought you two would be out shopping all morning. What, you didn't see what you wanted?"

Deborah shook her head as she reached for the cane she had set leaning against the wall. With her other hand, she picked up a large folder that Nicole had not noticed. "Gwen had an appointment to keep. I just needed her to run me to the bank to take care of a matter," Deborah said. "Come, sit with me. There's something I need to talk with you about."

"Okay," Nicole said as she followed her back to the family room. Deborah made her way to the breakfast table and sat down. She patted the chair next to her for Nicole to join her. Bewildered, Nicole did so, confused at what Deborah could possibly be up to.

"Nicole, I had Gwen take me to the bank. There was something I needed to get out my safe deposit box." Deborah stopped and slid the large envelope across the top of the table to Nicole.

Nicole looked from the envelope back over to Deborah, her eyes filled with questions. Deborah leaned forward and took Nicole's hand in hers as she said, "This is Marc's life insurance policy."

"I don't understand," Nicole said slowly.

"Nicole, your name is listed as the benefactor of his policy."

"What? No," Nicole stammered as she shook her head. "There has to be a mistake. Marc and I have been separated for five years. He ... I ... no ..."

"Nicole, listen to me," Deborah said softly as she leaned forward. "This is what Marc would have wanted. To have you and Abby taken care of would bring him such joy."

Nicole opened her mouth to protest, but nothing came out. She was literally speechless and could only look from Deborah to the envelope and back again.

"Marc would want you to have this," Deborah said softly but firmly. "Please, take it. It's yours."

Nicole carefully opened the envelope with shaky fingers. She slipped the paperwork out and started to read. All at once, Nicole's eyes got large as she saw the amount of the policy.

"I can't take this, Deborah. This is too much! You should have this."

Deborah shook her head as she smiled at the young woman in front of her. "Lee left me very well taken care of. This is yours. It's what Marc would want."

"What about Tyler?" Nicole asked. "There is no way he is going to let this happen without a fight."

Deborah was shaking her head before the words were out of Nicole's lips. "Tyler will be well taken care of when I go. Besides, I've had a long overdue talk with Tyler. He won't be bothering you anymore. You have my word."

"Really?" she asked in disbelief.

"Well, I don't expect him to give you a warm embrace at Thanksgiving dinner, but I think he'll come around. He just needs a little time and a lot of prayer," Deborah said with a wistful smile.

"I can definitely help with the prayer part. As a matter of fact, I'll ask Kathee to add Tyler to our prayer circle back home."

Deborah grew quiet and looked away from Nicole. Her hand trembled as she pulled it out of the younger woman's hand and placed it in her lap.

"What's wrong?" Nicole asked, confused at Deborah's sudden change in behavior.

Deborah looked over at her, and her lower lip trembled as she said, "You said home. I … I guess I was thinking that this was your home."

"Oh, Deborah," Nicole said, putting her arm around her. Their lives were so intertwined that it was hard to differentiate between their life now and their life before. "I'm sorry. I should have said something. I guess I have been thinking about Abby's and my future now that you are doing so much better. The truth is, you aren't going to need me here much longer, so I have been putting some applications out back home. I've actually had two phone interviews this week with a pediatrician's office that sounds very promising. They want me to come next week for a face-to-face interview."

Deborah leaned forward and clasped both of Nicole's hands in her own. "Don't let a silly old woman ruin your joy. You're right—you and Abby deserve to start your life, and if that's back in Maryland, then that's where you need to go. I am just so thankful that you came into my life when you did. The Lord saw fit to work it out so that I would heal both physically and spiritually, and He used you to do that. Thank you, dear child, for listening to Him and not running when I gave you every reason to."

"It's strange, but I feel as though this is my home, and …" Nicole paused as emotion overtook her. "And that you are my family too."

"Oh, dear child," Deborah said as she pulled her into a tight hug. "You are family, and no distance will ever change that."

After a few minutes, Deborah pulled back from Nicole with a chuckle.

"What?" Nicole asked, her eyebrows raised.

"I haven't had a chance to tell you my decision. I've decided to put the house up for sale. There's a new senior complex going up not far from church, and I'm buying a condo there."

"That's great! Isn't it?" Nicole asked, not sure how she felt. "I mean, you're okay with leaving this place, all the memories?"

"Yes, there are plenty of memories, but it really is too much for me to take care of anymore. Besides, I can make new memories at this place. It's got two bedrooms, so there's more than enough room for you and Abby to come visit."

"I think that's great," Nicole said as she soaked in the news. "I can help you pack before I go if you want."

"How about a large garage sale?" Deborah said as she laughed. "Outside of a few pieces of furniture and family memorabilia, I am not taking much with me. It's time to do some serious downsizing!"

Nicole joined her in laughter. "Well, I can help you with either. Just let me know."

"Thanks. That means a lot," Deborah said as she patted Nicole's knee. "Now, we need to take care of that life insurance policy for you. I got all the papers you will need. I've already called the insurance agent, and they are going to meet with you tomorrow morning."

"This is too unreal, Deborah," Nicole said with a shake of her head.

"Well, I for one couldn't be more excited for you. You have been such a blessing to me, Nicole. It's nice to know that you won't have to struggle financially. Marc is still taking care of you."

"Thanks, Deborah," Nicole said as she gestured to the envelope in front of her. "I am without words."

Deborah pulled her into an embrace as she spoke. "When you're family, you don't need words."

Chapter 28

"I can't believe Deborah sold her house in three days!" Nicole stated, still in a state of shock with how quickly everything had happened.

Gwen muttered her agreement as she reached around Nicole and grabbed a box next to her. Pulling out stacks of dishes, she started arranging them on a table that they had set up in the garage. In a few hours, they would be opening the garage sale. Deborah had determined that they would do it for one day only and whatever didn't get sold would go to a local charity.

"I cannot believe how much stuff she has," Gwen mumbled. "I think we need a bulldozer."

"I heard that," Deborah said as she walked down the two steps from the kitchen to the garage. Gwen groaned when she saw the large box she was carrying in her arms.

"Seriously, Deborah," she said as she went to help. "I think you're a closet hoarder. Did you throw anything away all the years you and Lee were married? Because I don't think so."

"It is surprising what you accumulate after forty-two years of marriage. I had no idea."

"Well, I hope we sell a lot of this stuff," Nicole said as she folded in the ends of the box she had just emptied and placed it under the table out of the way.

"Yes, me too," Gwen said as she dove into the last box and pulled its contents onto a table, "because there is not enough room at my place for you and all this."

Deborah chuckled as she stood with her hands on her hips and surveyed her garage. Her condo wouldn't be ready for another six weeks, so Deborah would be staying with her friend until it was ready.

"Don't worry about that," Deborah reassured Gwen. "I'm putting all the stuff I am keeping in a storage unit. The rest is going to charity. None of it is going to your place."

"Whew, that's a relief," Gwen said as she finished placing the last items on the table. "Let's get the signs out, and we'll be open for business."

"Did you shut the garage door?" Deborah asked as she lay back exhausted into the recliner.

"What garage?" Gwen drawled. "I think we sold that too."

Nicole chuckled as she threw herself on the couch next to Gwen. "I didn't think they would ever stop coming. It was crazy!"

"Yes, I was pleasantly surprised too. There's very little to pack up, but not tonight," Deborah said as she leaned the recliner all the way back. "When is Abby getting dropped off?"

"Not until tomorrow morning. Janet is bringing her home in the morning sometime. Abby and Charlotte have become inseparable since they met at Vacation Bible School."

"You've both made some good friends since you've been here."

"Yes, we have," Nicole said as she looked at the two ladies, "but you two are the best thing that's happened to me and Abby."

"Well, that goes both ways," Deborah said, her throat tightening.

"Nicole, there's a bottle of white wine in the cupboard above the stove. I think we deserve a glass tonight. Do you want to do the honors?"

"I would love to," Nicole said as she stretched and raised herself off the couch. "I can't believe some of those people. There was the one guy who wanted to haggle over everything! Unbelievable."

"Oh, yeah," Gwen agreed. "I was ready to tell him where he could take his business. People expect you to just give it to them for nothing! I'm exhausted! Please promise me that we are never going to do this again."

"Well, despite all that, we did do quite well," Deborah said with a happy sigh, "and we got rid of most everything. So much better than I had hoped."

Nicole walked into the family room with two tall glasses of wine and handed one to each lady before going to retrieve hers. She sank back down into the deep sofa with a sigh of contentment as she said, "This feels so good. I don't think I've ever worked so hard in my life. Those people were merciless."

"Well, it's done and, thanks to both of you, a great success," Deborah said as she lifted her glass to the two across from her. Nicole and Gwen raised their glasses before each took a long sip.

"Have either of you heard from Reese since he left?" Deborah asked as she swirled the glass softly in her hand.

"No," Nicole said wistfully. "We should call him and see how he is doing."

"Honestly," Gwen said as she eyed Nicole over the top of her glass, "I thought there might be something between you and Reese."

Nicole shook her head slowly as she said, "Reese was Marc's best friend. I never saw him as anything but that."

They were all silent in their own thoughts as they slowly sipped their wine.

"Nicole?" Gwen finally asked. "Deborah told me about your phone interview. I haven't had a chance to ask you about it with the garage sale and everything else."

"It went good. They want me to come next week for a face-to-face interview."

"Really? That's great!" Gwen said as she reached over and patted Nicole's knee. "You'll get it. I can just feel it."

"I hope you're right. It would definitely be an answer to prayer."

"When is the interview?" Deborah asked, trying to sound upbeat.

"Tuesday afternoon."

"When is your doctor appointment next week, Deborah?" Gwen asked.

"It's Wednesday afternoon, but I can always reschedule it if I need to."

"Let me check my schedule tomorrow at work and see if I can take the afternoon off to take you."

"Oh no, I can take her," Nicole said with a shake of her head. "I should be back in plenty of time for that."

"Are you sure?" Deborah asked. "You and Abby will be tired after your long ride back."

"We'll be fine. I may even come home Tuesday night after the interview."

"Well, then," Gwen said as she lifted her glass, "how about one last toast before we all turn in for the night? Here's to a great day, friends who are always there no matter what, and an exciting future for each of us."

"Hear, hear!" Nicole and Deborah chimed in and laughed as they clicked their glasses with Gwen's.

Chapter 29

Nicole flipped the magazine pages that she had lying in her lap but her mind wasn't on the gorgeous models that were in the full-page ads or on the latest scandal in a celebrities' divorce in Hollywood. Her mind had been in a whirlwind since the call she had gotten this morning from the pediatrician's office where she had had her interview the day before. The interview had gone well, really well, and this morning they had called and made her a formal offer.

The money was going to be a little less than she had hoped for, but she realized that she was just starting, fresh out of school; it was to be expected. Besides, with the insurance money from Marc, it would be enough for her and Abby to get a small place of their own.

"Ms. Brennan."

It took a second for Nicole to realize that Dr. Thiel was standing in the doorway that led to the back of the office. Hastily, she threw the magazine down next to her and made her way across the well-maintained reception area. Fear gnawed at her stomach as she approached the doctor, wondering what was wrong, but the doctor greeted her with a reassuring smile,

"Deborah is fine," he said softly as they stepped into the hallway and shut the door behind them. "As a matter of fact, she's doing remarkably well. My PA is doing a final assessment on her now, but I wanted to speak with you for a moment."

"Sure," Nicole said, relief rolling off her shoulders. "What can I help you with?"

Dr. Thiel pointed down the hall with his arm as he said, "How about we talk in my office?"

Nicole nodded her head and followed the doctor down the hall and into his office. She was surprised at how small it was. Every inch was taken up with bookshelves and a large oversized desk, but it managed not to feel cramped.

A nurse grabbed the doctor's attention as he had started to enter, and for a time, he was out in the hall discussing something in a lowered voice. After a minute, he apologized as he shut the door, made his way to his chair, and sat down across from Nicole.

Nicole smiled as she held her hands tightly in her lap. She had been trying to figure out what Dr. Thiel wanted to discuss with her. He had said Deborah was doing well, but there must be something that concerned him; why else was she here?

"First, I want to tell you what a fine job you have done," Dr. Thiel began as he leaned his elbows on the desk, hands clasped together. "Quite honestly, I didn't give Deborah much of a chance of a full recovery. Mostly because she seemed to have given up, and I find when a patient loses the will to fight, then they don't usually recover. I don't know what you did, but you gave her that will to fight, and because of that, she has surpassed even my expectations."

Nicole opened her mouth to protest, but Dr. Theil held up his hand and stopped her. He mulled something over as he stared at her. Finally, he said, "I understand that you got a job offer this morning from a doctor's office back where you are from."

"Yes," she said, confused at the change in topic. "It's at a pediatrician's office. They called and made me an offer this morning."

"I'm going to be quite honest. I have been impressed with how well you handled the whole situation with Deborah. I saw the difference in her with each appointment." Dr. Theil folded his arms in front of him and leaned forward as he continued, "I think we may be able to find you work here, if you want to stay. I have some connections, and there are a couple openings that I think you would be well suited for. One is in cardiac, and the other is ER. Both would be a good fit for you, I think. I can set up interviews for you, if you'd like, with both departments, and you can decide after that."

"I'm ... I'm at a loss for words," Nicole stammered. "This is incredible."

"Well, I don't want to lose good people, and I think you will be an asset to this hospital."

"Thank you," Nicole said, stunned by the turn of events. "I would love to interview for either of the positions."

"Great!" Dr. Theil said as he stood and shook her hand. "We got your information, and I will get the ball rolling. You should expect to hear from them in the next day or two."

Deborah was sitting out in the waiting room when Nicole came out. She raised her eyebrows at Nicole as she walked across the waiting area, but Nicole decided not to tell Deborah the real reason Dr. Theil had wanted to see her. She didn't want to get her hopes up on something that might or might not happen.

"What did the doctor want to see you about?" Deborah asked.

"Just wanted a report on your therapy and how it was going. He's quite pleased with your progress."

"Humph ..." Deborah muttered as she stood and took Nicole's extended arm. "That's all he talked about during my appointment too. Don't know why he's so surprised."

Nicole smiled to herself as they made their way out to her car. "You want to stop at Big Boy on the way home? We can split a strawberry shortcake, if you like."

"That sounds good," Deborah agreed with a nod of her head.

Nicole helped get her buckled in before shutting the door and making her way around the back of the car to the other side. She took a moment to smile and let what Dr. Theil had offered her sink in again before sliding into the driver's seat and starting up the car.

"I can't believe he offered you a job! That's amazing, Nicole!"

Nicole had been bursting to talk to Kathee as soon as she had gotten the offer from Dr. Theil. She had made idle chatter all the way home with Deborah and had called her friend as soon as she could get away to the privacy of her room.

"I know," she said as she leaned back in her bed, her arm draped over her eyes. "I don't know what to do, Kathee. I really don't."

"Sounds like this doctor must think a lot of you to make you an offer to work at the hospital there. That says a lot about you and how you handled this whole situation with Deborah. Others saw your example; Deborah's doctor noticed. I'm so proud of you, Nicole. I can see how you have grown through this whole experience."

"Thanks, Kathee, but that doesn't help me with my decision. What do I do? I have one job offer and two more interviews. I can't believe this! How do I choose?"

"Such a problem to have," her friend teased.

"Yes, you're right. I know this is a good problem. I just needed to tell someone."

"Well, I'm glad you thought of me, but I think there's someone else you need to be talking to, don't you agree?"

"I knew you'd set me straight," Nicole said with a chuckle.

"Just remember to listen to that small voice. He'll never let you down."

"Yes, you're right. Thanks, Kathee, I'll talk to you later. Bye."

Nicole hit *end* and set her phone on the bedside next to her as she slid to her knees on the floor next to the bed. She folded her hands and rested her elbows on the edge of the bed as she lifted her eyes. Then she spent time inquiring of the Lord what was on her heart and opening her heart in return to what He had to say.

Chapter 30

Nicole nervously fussed with the spray of flowers she had picked from Deborah's garden as she arranged them in the crystal vase and set them in the center of the kitchen table. She stepped back and assessed them. Satisfied, she let her eyes wander across the family room.

It was surreal to realize that tonight would be their last night in this house. Tomorrow, movers would be here to pack it up and move it out. Some of it was going to Gwen's, where Deborah would be residing until her condo at the senior center was finished, and the rest would be going to a storage unit for the time being.

Nicole had rented a small U-Haul for her and Abby's meager belongings. Deborah had insisted that she take the twin bed and dresser from Marc's room for Abby, and she had given Nicole the small breakfast table.

"I want you to have something of me with you," Deborah had said with a quiver in her lip the night before.

Nicole felt almost guilty for not telling Deborah her decision, but she wanted it to be a surprise. Gwen had come that morning and taken Deborah up to sign the final papers for her condo. When they were done, they were coming back, and Nicole was planning on showing, rather than telling, them the surprise. "Mommy ... can I wear this?"

Nicole shook the thoughts out her head as she turned her focus on her daughter. Abby's cast had finally come off a few days before, and she now stood in front of her dressed in a Cinderella dress and slippers that she had gotten for dress-up.

Nicole suppressed a smile as she exclaimed, "Why look at you, Miss Abigail Brennan. You are the prettiest princess I have ever seen. Come give your mommy a hug!"

Abby giggled as she ran into her mother's outstretched arms. She looked expectantly at Nicole's face and asked again, "Can I we wear Cinderella to show Gramma our surprise?"

"Of course you can, sweetie. That would be perfect. Let's go upstairs and do your hair up like a princess, okay?"

Abby nodded her head eagerly as she grabbed Nicole's hand and started to pull her down the hall toward the stairway. Nicole could only laugh as she let her daughter drag her along. Abby was as eager as Nicole to surprise Deborah with their news. They had laid out their "top secret" plans late into the evening the night before after a busy couple of weeks. Nicole didn't think Abby would be able to keep their surprise secret for very much longer, but she wasn't alone. Today was going to be so exciting!

"Come on, Abby," she said as she scooped her laughing daughter into her arms and ran up the stairs. "You're such a slowpoke! Grandma and Aunt Gwen will be here any minute! We need to be ready for them!"

"I am so tired," Deborah complained as she turned the key in the front door and pushed it open. "I had no idea how much work and effort all this would take. What was I thinking?"

"It's almost over," Gwen consoled her friend as she followed her in and shut the door behind them. "In a few months, this will be a distant memory and you will be so happy in your new home."

"I hope you're right." Deborah stopped short as she saw Nicole and Abby standing in front of her at the base of the stairs. Both wore a funny expression on their faces, and Abby was dressed in her Cinderella outfit with a tiny braid down one side of her hair.

"What's this?" she asked as she leaned over and looked at Abby. "Is there a ball tonight that no one told me about?"

Abby put both tiny hands over her mouth and giggled as she looked up at her mother. Nicole put her arm around her daughter and drew her close to her side as she said, "No ball, but we would like to take you ladies on a special ride. We have a surprise to share with you on our last night together."

Deborah raised an eyebrow at Nicole and then looked over her shoulder at Gwen. "You know anything about this?" she asked.

"Nope," Gwen said with raised hands. "I'm as much in the dark as you are."

"Come on, Gramma!" Abby said as she grabbed her hand. She turned excited eyes to Nicole as she exclaimed, "I want to show Gramma our new car, Mommy!"

"New car?" Deborah looked up from Abby to Nicole and smiled. "Well, let's not stand around here. I want to see this!"

"It's in the garage!" Abby yelled as she started to pull Deborah along. "Come on, Aunt Gwen! You can see our new car too!"

"Well, I thought you'd never ask," Gwen replied as she got in line behind everyone else. Nicole managed to get ahead of her daughter in time to open the door to the garage and flick on the light.

"What do you think?" she asked.

"Nice," Gwen said as she stepped around the others and went to stand by the white Lexus SUV. "Very nice."

"Why, yes, it is," Deborah agreed as she smiled over at Nicole. "When did you get this?"

"This morning," Nicole replied, glancing nervously over at Deborah. "I went to the dealership yesterday after Abby left for school and test-drove a couple of cars and decided on this. Then I went to the bank this morning and got the money from the annuity Marc left me and Abby, and I picked it up as soon as she got home today."

Deborah looked over at her with a smile and said, "I am so happy you did that. I feel so much better with you having a good, safe, and reliable car. I was afraid every time you drove your old car that you would get stranded somewhere. I know that Marc would be happy too."

Relaxing her shoulders, Nicole let out a sigh of relief. "Thanks, I was a little nervous about how you would feel about this."

"Oh, I agree with Deborah," Gwen added as she walked around to the other side of the Lexus. "This is a great car for you and Abby. I'll feel better too, knowing you're driving this."

"Thanks," Nicole said. Then she motioned toward the car. "Who wants to go for a ride?"

"Me! Me! Me!" Abby exclaimed, jumping up and down in excitement.

All three women laughed as Nicole said, "Well, okay, then. Gwen, you want to ride in back with Abby, and Deborah can ride up front with me?"

"Sounds good to me," Gwen said as she opened the back passenger door and slid in. Nicole got Abby buckled into her booster seat while Deborah settled herself into the front passenger seat. Nicole slid behind the driver's wheel, buckled up, and after seeing that everyone else was secure, opened the garage door and backed out. A few minutes later, Nicole entered the on-ramp to the expressway and merged with the oncoming traffic.

"This drives nice," Deborah commented as she looked over the front console. "I can't believe the technology they have in these cars now."

"Yes," Nicole agreed as she kept her eye on the traffic. "There's a back-up camera and lane change warner in case there's a car in my blind spot. I like that feature the best."

"It's really comfortable too," Gwenn added, leaning forward so they could hear her. "Even back here."

Nicole saw the exit ramp she wanted and put her blinker on. A few minutes later, she made another turn down a quiet street of older, well-kept homes.

"This will be so nice for your trip back," Deborah said as Nicole pulled up in front of a cute Cape Cod and parked. Deborah looked at Nicole in confusion and asked, "What are we doing here?"

Nicole couldn't hide her joy any longer as a smile lit up her face. "Deborah, Abby and I are not moving back to Maryland."

"What?" Deborah said, her face clouded in confusion.

Gwen leaned forward and gripped Deborah's shoulder as she looked over at Nicole and said, "I think what Nicole is trying to tell us is that they aren't leaving."

Nicole nodded as she spoke. "Dr. Theil offered me a job at the hospital, and I accepted. I am going to be working in the cardiac and stroke rehab department. The hours are great—no nights, no weekends, and no holidays. Plus, I got a sign-on bonus, and the salary I will be making is going to be more than enough for me to get this house."

Deborah looked from Nicole to the small Cape Cod they sat in front of, and the realization hit her. She turned back to Nicole and asked, "Is this it? Is this your new home?"

Nicole smiled as she nodded her head. "Yes, it's ours—Abby's and mine."

"Oh!" Deborah exclaimed as she reached across the console to give Nicole a hug.

"I want to go inside, Mommy!" Abby said as she struggled against the seatbelt constraints.

"Can we?" Gwen asked, getting as excited as Abby. "We can at least look in the windows. It doesn't look like there's anyone living in it."

"It is unoccupied, but we don't have to look in the windows," Nicole stated as she stepped out of the car and held up a set of house keys between her fingers. "Who wants to see our new home?"

"Well, you don't have to ask me twice," Gwen said as she opened her door and stepped out.

Nicole got Abby unhooked from her seatbelt, lifted her down, and took her hand. They walked over to join Gwen and Deborah, who stood on the sidewalk looking at her and Abby's new home.

"Shall we?" she asked as she started up the short walk to her front door. A few minutes later, they were standing in the middle of the front living room.

"What do you think?" Nicole asked, her nerves getting the better of her. This had been such a big move for her, and it hadn't been easy. She and her realtor had hit the pavement for days going through homes, and she had about given up on finding the right one when they had walked into this one. Immediately, Nicole had known this was the one. Now she needed to hear confirmation that she had made the right choice from the one person who had come to mean the world to her.

Deborah walked around the perimeter of the cozy living room, taking in the crown molding and quaint fireplace, before turning to Nicole with a smile. "I think you did good, Nicole. I am so happy for you. I'm just overwhelmed at all of this."

"You're not alone. I thought for sure Abby and I were headed back to Maryland and I would be working in a pediatrician's office, but then I took you to your appointment with Dr. Theil, and he made me an offer that I knew had to come from God." Nicole paused as tears choked her. Swallowing them down, she reached over and took the older woman's hands in her own and said, "You see, I didn't want to leave you, Deborah. You're my family now."

Deborah didn't speak as tears filled her own eyes. Reaching over, she pulled Nicole into a tight hug as they let the tears fall. After a few minutes, they pulled away, each wiping the tears away with the back of their hands until Gwen handed them some Kleenex she had pulled out of her purse.

"Abby," Gwen said as she took the little girl's hand, "why don't you give me a private tour of your new home?"

A few minutes later, Nicole and Deborah were alone as Abby dragged Gwen upstairs to see her bedroom. Nicole took Deborah by the hand as she led her to the dining area, which was connected to the living room by a large, arched opening.

Deborah took in the quaint home as Nicole led her into the dining area. Like the living room, it too had the crown molding along the ceiling. "This is so lovely, Nicole," Deborah said as she turned around in the middle of the room. "I can see you making this a warm and loving home for you and Abby."

Nicole hugged herself as she chewed her lower lip. Deborah touched Nicole's hand, drawing the younger woman's eyes up to her own.

"It's okay, Nicole," she said softly. "Marc would want this for you and Abby." She leaned in closer as she added, "I want this for you and Abby."

"Thanks," Nicole said softly. "That means more than you know. It's important to me that you believe I am being smart with Marc's money. I used some of it for the down payment."

Deborah took a step back in surprise as she said, "Well, no one can say you haven't been. You put the bulk of it in a trust for Abby, and using the money to buy this house and the car are smart investments.

"I do think you should take some of that money and spoil yourself a little," she added. "No one would fault you for it, and even if they did, so what? This is your money, Nicole, and you do with it what you want. You certainly have earned it."

Nicole chuckled as she said, "Well, maybe I could go get a manicure. You could watch Abby for me, since we're going to be so close to each other."

"We are?" Deborah said, looking around. All at once, her eyes shot up as realization hit her. "My condo?"

"We're only a few blocks apart," Nicole said as a smile lit her face. "The church and your condo are just around the corner. We can visit each other as often as we want."

"Oh, my," Deborah said as she looked out the bay window and tried to get her bearings. "I've never been good with directions, and I was so busy admiring your car that I never paid attention where we were at."

"That was a bonus when I saw this place. I knew as soon as I walked in that this was going to be our new home."

Tears filled Deborah's eyes as she turned her head away. Alarmed, Nicole touched the older woman's arm and said, "I'm sorry, Deborah—I thought you would be happy we were going to be staying and living so close. I should have asked you first, but I wanted to …"

"Shhh," Deborah said as she put her fingers to Nicole's lips. A smile broke through her tears as she said, "There is nothing that would make me happier, sweet child. I have grown to love you and Abby, and it was breaking my heart that I would be losing you two. I am just so overcome with joy that I can't hide it. These are tears of joy, Nicole, not distress. This is what I've been praying for, and He answered my prayers. I am happy beyond words."

Nicole gathered Deborah in a hug as they laughed and cried together. After a few minutes, Deborah pulled herself away as she wiped her eyes with the back of her hand.

"When do you and Abby move in?" she asked.

"We're moving in tomorrow," Nicole replied as she wiped her eyes too. "My realtor was able to get it pushed through, and I closed on it yesterday. I went to the dealership right after and picked out my car."

"Really?" Deborah said in surprise. "You had a busy afternoon yesterday."

"I know," Nicole said with a smile. "God has been so good to us."

"Yes, He has," Deborah said and then patted Nicole's arm. "There's just one thing."

"What's that?" Nicole asked.

"Well, I know that I told you that you could have the breakfast table set, but I think I've changed my mind."

"Oh, that's okay, Deborah," Nicole quickly stammered. "That was nice of you to even offer …"

Deborah raised her hand to stop her. "I don't want you to have it because I think the dining room set would look so much nicer in here."

Nicole's mouth fell open as she stumbled over her words. "But … that's a family heirloom … I can't … Tyler should have it …"

Deborah took Nicole gently by the shoulders and waited until she was done before she spoke. "I have no room in the condo, and Tyler is more into the modern, sleek look. Marc was the only one who truly treasured that piece. I was going to sell them at the auction with all the rest of the furnishings that are left."

Deborah paused as tears filled the brim of her eyes. She forced the tears back as she looked at Nicole with tender love and said, "You are family, Nicole. I know that you will treasure them. I want you to have the table, Nicole."

Nicole did not stop the tears as they ran down her cheeks. She smiled as she threw herself into the older woman's arms.

"I would be honored to have it," she said, her words muffled against Deborah's shoulder.

"Good, then it's settled. Now I want to see the rest of your place." Deborah started to move but paused when she saw a look come over Nicole's face.

"What is it?" she asked gently.

Nicole looked down at her hands a second before raising them to meet Deborah's and said, "I don't know what to tell Abby about her father. She is going to ask about it someday, and I don't know what I'm going to tell her. I'm so ashamed of what I did, and I don't want that to be her burden too. A part of me wants to tell her that Marc is her daddy, but that would be a lie, and I don't want to lie to her either." Nicole looked away as her throat tightened.

Reaching over, Deborah put her hand under Nicole's chin. Gently, she raised Nicole's face until their eyes met and with tender words, Deborah spoke. "You tell Abby the truth. You tell her that her daddy loved her from the moment he heard about her. You tell her that he wanted nothing more than to come home and be a family with both of you, but that Jesus needed him to go home to heaven instead."

Nicole's eyes brimmed over with gratitude as she whispered, "Thank you."

"No need to thank me. You know how much I love that precious girl. I don't know where I would be if the Lord hadn't brought both of you into my life when He did."

Nicole smiled as she patted Deborah's hand and said, "How about we finish the tour? Abby has probably talked poor Gwen's ear off."

"Sounds good to me," Deborah agreed as she rose and followed Nicole to the open staircase off the living room. A smile touched her lips as she followed Nicole upstairs. Silently, she lifted her eyes to heaven and whispered a prayer of thanks.

Chapter 31

Nicole pushed the wooden screen door open with one hand as she balanced a cup of hot tea in the other. She paused as she stood with the door open and peered into the living room behind her.

"Come on out if you're coming," she called into the house.

Back in the shadow of the dining room, she could make out a soft yellow tail as it wagged. A few seconds later, a small yellow lab timidly joined her at the door.

"Come on out, Samson," she said as she gently nudged him with her foot. Being careful not to step on or trip over the puppy, Nicole made her way over to a glider and sat down. She wrapped both hands around her cup and took a sip as she pushed the glider with the toes of her shoes. Samson went to his usual spot and sat at the corner of the porch, looking out down the street.

Nicole smiled as she watched the lab sitting so loyally, waiting for Abby to come home. He had been a housewarming gift from Gwen and Deborah, and he had immediately won her heart. She had let her daughter name the puppy, and it had just so happened that the story in Sunday school that week had been on Samson. So, Samson was what Abby had declared his name would be.

"You'll have to grow into your name a little bit more," Nicole said softly to the puppy. Samson looked up at her and then turned back and continued his vigil.

Nicole relaxed as a soft breeze blew across the porch, stirring up leaves in its way. Samson's head came up, and his ears perked as he watched the leaves dance across the lawn.

"Stay, Samson," she said firmly. The yellow lab looked up at her for a minute before stretching out and resting his head on his front paws. Nicole closed her eyes and leaned back as she breathed in deeply. She had always loved the smell of autumn.

She let her mind reflect back on her day at work. She had learned that afternoon that a dear patient who had been in cardiac rehab for a month had passed away after suffering another heart attack. Eleanor had been one of Nicole's favorites. She had showed a lot of spunk and hadn't let her condition slow her down one bit. She had come to every class energized and ready to work out. Nicole loved her job, but days like this were hard.

She opened her eyes as Samson let out a bark and started prancing at her feet. A car that Nicole did not recognize pulled into the driveway. Nicole gently shushed the puppy as she stood and walked over to the top of the steps. The driver's door opened, and Nicole took in a deep breath as Tyler stepped out.

Tyler paused as he looked up at her; then he made his way up the walk to where she stood. Nicole tried to unclench her stomach as she watched him make his way to her, questions burning in her head. Squaring her shoulders, Nicole straightened her stance as she held his eyes.

"Hi, Nicole," Tyler said as he put one foot on the bottom step and looked up at her.

"I wasn't expecting to see you, Tyler," Nicole said calmly.

"I know," Tyler said, his dark eyes holding hers. "I know that I haven't been exactly supportive."

"No, more like downright mean and judgmental," Nicole stated, folding her arms in front of her.

Tyler took another step up as Nicole held her spot. She was not going to let Tyler intimidate her anymore, and definitely not in her home. At the moment, she was thankful that Abby was with Deborah, but she knew that they could come walking up the street anytime. Whatever Tyler wanted to say, she didn't really care.

"You don't need to come any further, Tyler. You can say what you came here to say from there."

Tyler lowered his gaze a moment and then turned it back up to Nicole. Nicole almost took a step backward when she saw the look of remorse in his eyes.

"I just came to say that I'm sorry, Nicole, for how I treated you. I said some awful things, I know. Since Mom called and talked to me, I've been thinking a lot about Marc. Believe it or not, I miss my brother."

Tyler paused as he choked down tears. His eyes were glistening when he looked back up at her. "I know deep in my heart that if Marc was still here, he would have wanted to start over with you. I know this because he told me himself before he left for his last deployment. He never gave up on you, Nicole."

Nicole took a step back as Tyler's words sank in. She felt her knees bend as she turned to sit. Tyler was at Nicole's side and held her gently by her elbow as he guided her to the wooden glider. He helped her sit and sat on the edge next to her.

"Can I get you something?" he asked, concern clouding his eyes.

"No, I'm okay … I just … I …" Nicole's hand shook as she absently reached to push a strand of hair out of her eye.

"What is it, Nicole?" Tyler gently nudged.

"It's just," Nicole began and then looked at Tyler. "I can't believe that Marc … he forgave me before … he got my letter." Unable to stop the tears, Nicole put both hands over her eyes and cried.

Not knowing what else to do, Tyler folded his hands in his lap and gazed down at them. "I came here to ask for your forgiveness,

Nicole," he said finally, raising his eyes back to her as tears started down his cheeks. "Can you ever forgive me?"

Nicole lifted her head and looked up at Tyler. Compassion washed over her as she reached over and took his hands in hers and said, "Of course I forgive you, Tyler."

She leaned her forehead against Tyler's as they shared a fresh onset of tears. Finally, Nicole pulled away and wiped her sleeve across her still-moist eyes. Tyler pulled a clean handkerchief out of a back pocket and offered it to her. She thanked him as she took it and finished drying her eyes. A timid bark came from under the glider. Tyler reached under and pulled up the small puppy.

"Well, hi, little guy," he said, lifting the small bundle of fur in the air. "I didn't know we had a visitor."

"This is Samson," Nicole said with a chuckle. "He's our newest addition."

"Well, hi, Samson," Tyler said. "You're going to grow into those oversized feet one day."

"Was Deborah expecting you?" Nicole asked as she stroked Samson's soft fur.

"No, this was kind of spur-of-the-moment," Tyler said with a shake of his head. "I woke up this morning with an overwhelming need to make this right. And I didn't want to do it over the phone. I needed to look you in the eyes so that you could see that I was sincere."

"So you hopped on a plane and flew all the way over here?" Nicole said, incredulous.

"Yes," Tyler said with a sheepish smile. "Sounds kind of crazy, I guess."

"No, I think it sounds about right. I know from personal experience that God works in many wonderful ways. I think He has been working in your heart, Tyler."

"Maybe," Tyler said as he looked down at the puppy nestled in his lap. Nicole could sense that he wasn't there yet, but she was sure that the Lord had Tyler in His hands, and she found comfort in that.

Standing, she looked at Tyler as she tilted her head and said,

"Deborah and Abby should be here anytime. You want to wait with me for them inside?"

Tyler nodded his head as he stood with Samson tucked under one arm and followed Nicole in.

Nicole and Tyler were seated at the dining room table, each nursing a hot cup of green tea. They had spent the past half hour reminiscing over Marc when they heard chatter from the front porch.

"Mommy!" Abby said with excitement as she barged through the front door. "Guess what Billy did!"

Deborah nearly walked into Abby when the girl came to an abrupt stop.

"Abby, what are you doing?" Deborah said. "You nearly ..." Deborah stopped when she saw her son seated next to Nicole.

"Hi, Mom," he said as he rose, walked over, and gave her a kiss on the cheek.

Abby leaned into Deborah, wrapping an arm tightly around the older woman's leg and looked warily up at Tyler. Nicole got up from the table and went over to her daughter. She squatted down next to her and stroked her arm as she said, "Hey, sweetie, how was your day?"

Abby just leaned into her mother, never taking her eyes off Tyler, and said, "I don't like him. He yelled at you."

"May I?" Tyler asked Nicole. Nicole gave a silent nod of her head as Tyler squatted next to her. He gave Abby a soft smile and said, "I know that the last time you saw me, I was angry at your mom."

Abby squeezed herself even closer to Deborah and nodded her head.

"I want you to know that I am sorry about what I did. It was wrong of me to say those things to your mommy, but most important, I am sorry that I scared you. Can you forgive me, Abby?"

Abby looked at her mom, and Nicole gave her a smile and said, "It's okay, Abby. Tyler has said he's sorry to me too, and I've forgiven him. You don't have to be afraid of him anymore."

Tyler leaned back on his heels as he studied Abby and then said, "I don't blame you for not trusting me, Abby. Trust needs to be earned. How about this—how about we take some time to get to know each other? Will you give me a chance to earn your trust and forgiveness?"

Abby seemed to roll the request around in her head before she gave him a nod.

"That's great," Tyler said as he smiled at her. "I'm looking forward to getting to know you better."

Nicole took Abby's hand as both she and Tyler stood and said, "Abby and I are going to go get her changed out of her school clothes. Why don't you and Deborah have a seat? We'll be down in a few minutes."

Deborah watched them make their way upstairs before turning to her son. "Why did I not know you were coming?"

"It was a spur-of-the-moment decision," Tyler said as he motioned for his mother to have a seat on the sofa. He took a seat on the edge of a chair opposite her and continued. "Ever since your call, I have been thinking about what you said."

Deborah raised an eyebrow in surprise as she said, "Really?"

"What you said to me, Mom, made me reevaluate my life, and I realized that I didn't like who I had become." Tyler leaned forward, his hands clasped in front of him as he continued, "I want to be the man that would have made Dad proud, and I want to be the son I ought to have been for you."

Deborah leaned forward and grasped her son's hands with hers. "I think you're doing a good job so far. I've never given up on you Tyler, not ever."

"I know, Mom. Thanks." Tyler tilted his head as he studied his mother a moment. "You look good, much better than the last time I saw you."

Deborah's hand unconsciously reached up to touch her hair. She had just started going back to her old hairstylists a few weeks ago and had gotten a cut and color.

"I do feel better," she admitted and then dropped her hand back into her lap. "But I have to tell you, Tyler, that it's more than my outward appearance that has changed. The Lord used my stroke to make me see that I couldn't do this alone. I needed Nicole and Gwen and Abby, but most importantly, I needed Him."

Tyler nodded his head and said, "I'm beginning to understand what you are saying, Mom. Believe it or not, a friend at work asked me to go with him to his church. I went last Sunday with him and his family."

"Oh, I am so happy to hear that," Deborah said as she leaned forward and touched her son's hand. "He can change your life if you let Him."

"Well, I think He may be already," Tyler said with a chuckle. "I'm here, aren't I? I never thought I could get to this point, but it feels like all that bitterness is gone. I really can't explain it."

"You don't have to," Deborah said with a smile. "I get it."

Tyler looked at his mom and nodded as he said, "Yes, I know you do."

Abby was still quiet when Nicole got her up to her room. Even Samson, who had followed them upstairs, couldn't get a reaction from her. Nicole sat on her daughter's brass canopied bed with its unicorn bedspread and pulled Abby into her lap.

"Want to talk to me?" she asked gently.

Abby put two fingers in her mouth and shook her head. Nicole let out a soft sigh and hugged her daughter, resting her chin on the top of her head. "You can tell me how you're feeling."

"He yelled at you and Gramma. He scared me."

"I know sweetie," Nicole said, squeezing her daughter closer as she prayed for wisdom. "That was a long time ago, and now he's sorry for what he's done."

She pulled her daughter away and turned her so she could look her in the eyes. She smiled as she pushed a piece of hair out of Abby's eyes that had escaped the barrette clasp on the side of her head. "Do you remember that we've been praying for Tyler?"

Abby nodded her head slowly.

"Don't you think that maybe Jesus answered our prayers?" Nicole asked softly.

"Yes," Abby replied, her eyes lighting up a little more. "My teacher says we should forgive people, even bad ones."

"Do you think that means we should forgive Tyler too?"

Abby thought it over for just a second before she nodded her head. She grabbed her play clothes off the bed where Nicole had laid them that morning and started to undress.

"Help me, Mommy!" she exclaimed when she struggled getting her shirt over her head.

"Slow down, pumpkin," Nicole said with a chuckle. "Grandma and Tyler aren't going anywhere."

Abby pushed her hair out of her eyes as Nicole finished helping her get dressed and asked, "Is Gramma Tyler's mommy?"

"Yes, sweetie, she is," Nicole said as she bent over to tie a shoe that had come undone.

"And Gramma is Daddy's mommy?"

"Uh-huh," Nicole said, still tying her daughter's shoe.

"Is he my uncle, then?" she asked.

Nicole sat up and leaned back on her knees. She didn't know why she had never thought that her daughter would figure out the connection. Now what?

She looked over her daughter's shoulder to the framed picture of Marc that Abby had on her dresser. He was squatted in full fatigues in front of his tank with a huge grin on his face. Nicole had had that picture on a shelf in the living room, and one afternoon after church, Abby had started asking questions that Nicole had known would come.

Gently, Nicole had taken the picture and sat her daughter down in her lap as she explained who Marc was and how much he had loved them and had wanted to be her daddy, but that Jesus needed him in heaven more. Abby had asked if she could have the picture of Marc for her room. Nicole smiled at the memory when Abby had taken the picture in her hands and called Marc her angel daddy.

"You know what?" she said as she gave her daughter a squeeze. "I think that we should ask Tyler that question."

Abby nodded her head in agreement and grabbed Nicole's hand as they started to head out the door. At the last second, Abby pulled away and ran to her dresser. She grabbed the picture of Marc and went back to her mom. Nicole smiled as they made their way downstairs.

Deborah and Tyler were talking softly when they heard Abby and Nicole making their way back down the stairs. Tyler stood as they got to the bottom and made their way to living area.

"Well, you look more comfortable, Abby," Deborah said. She raised her arm out as Abby came over and nestled herself by her side. Deborah gave her a quick squeeze and noticed that Abby was holding tightly to something at her side. "What do you have there, sweetie?"

Abby drew it tighter to her as she looked up at Tyler. Nicole came over to squat in front of her daughter.

"It's okay," she said softly. "You can show Tyler."

"What do you have there, Abby?" Tyler asked softly as he squatted in front of her.

"This is a picture of my daddy," Abby said as she held out the picture to show Tyler.

Tyler took the picture from Abby and studied it. Nicole sent up a quick prayer as she watched to see how Tyler would react. She didn't realize that she had been holding her breath until Tyler looked up at her with gentle understanding and a soft smile.

He turned his attention back to Abby and said, "Your daddy was a special man, Abby, and I know that he loved you and your mommy very much."

Abby reached her hand out and touched the tear that was running down Tyler's cheek. "Don't cry," she said. "Daddy is in heaven with Jesus."

"That's right, Abby," Tyler said. "Your daddy is in heaven."

"Reese said that my daddy was very brave."

Tyler glanced up at Nicole and his mother with a raised eyebrow.

"Reese was with Marc over there. He came to visit after he got back," Nicole explained with a soft smile.

Tyler nodded his head as he swallowed down the tears that were choking him and turned his attention back to Abby.

"Do you want to be my uncle?" Abby asked as she studied him closely.

"Yes, Abby, I would love to be your uncle," Tyler said as he put his arm around the little girl and pulled her close.

Deborah looked incredulously over their heads at Nicole, who smiled broadly back.

God is good, she mouthed. Deborah smiled and nodded her head in agreement.

"Come on, you two," Nicole said, squeezing Tyler's shoulder lightly as he and Abby pulled apart. "How long can you stay, Tyler?"

"I have to be back for a meeting tomorrow morning. My flight leaves tonight around eight."

"Good," Nicole said. "You can stay and have dinner with us."

"We're having tacos!" Abby exclaimed, beaming up at Tyler.

Nicole laughed and said, "Abby's favorite meal, if you haven't figured that out, and there's plenty. You're more than welcome to stay."

"Please stay, Uncle Tyler!" Abby chirped, bouncing up and down as she grabbed his hand.

Tyler laughed as he reached down and picked the little girl up. "How did you know that tacos were my favorite meal too?"

Abby looked over at Deborah for confirmation, and Deborah held up both hands as she said, "Yes, they were, and he made a royal mess each time we had them."

"That's great!" Nicole said as she stood. "I'll get them ready, then."

"Can I help?" Tyler asked.

"No, you sit down and relax. I got this."

"I can help you, Nicole," Deborah offered. As she stood, she turned to her son and said, "You can get to know your niece a little bit more."

Tyler nodded his head as he looked over at Abby, who was now seated next to him on the sofa, and said, "I think that's a great idea." Deborah smiled at the two of them before turning to make her way through the dining room and into the kitchen tucked away in the back of the house. Nicole was leaning against the far counter when Deborah walked in.

Both women looked at each other a moment in silence before Nicole said in a soft whisper, "Can you believe it?"

"No," Deborah said quietly with a shake of her head. "But we serve an awesome God, don't we?"

Nicole nodded her head in agreement as she pushed away from the counter and threw her arms around Deborah. Deborah squeezed her tightly as they rejoiced together.

Epilogue

"**M**ommy, they're here! Aunt Gwen and Gramma are here!" Abby danced around her as Nicole took a look in the oven to check on the progress of the turkey. Satisfied that everything was coming along fine, she turned and followed her daughter, who had already reached the front door and opened it.

"Well, hi there, missy. Where's the fire?"

Nicole smiled as she stretched out her hands and took the dish that Gwen was holding.

"This girl has been bothering me all morning asking when you two were going to get here."

"Well, where's my hug?" Deborah said as she set a dish down on the table by the door and held out her arms. Abby threw her arms around Deborah and gave her a huge squeeze.

Gwen laughed as she shrugged her coat off and hung it up in the small hall closet. Turning, she helped Deborah with hers and hung it up next to her own.

"Your house is adorable!" Gwen said as she stood and took in the living and dining room.

Nicole had enjoyed decorating her home for the fall season. It was one of her favorite times of the year. "Thanks. Abby and I had fun going to the cider mill a few weeks ago with her class."

"We went on a hayride and got to pick some pumpkins!" Abby chimed in.

"I saw the pumpkins and hay stalks on your front porch!" Deborah said. "You did a very nice job!"

"Thanks. Here, let me get these to the kitchen," Nicole said as she grabbed the dish Deborah had set down and reached for Gwen's with her free hand.

"I got it," Gwen said as she took the dish and followed Nicole. She set hers on the kitchen counter and said, "Mine will just have to be warmed up."

Nicole peeked under the foil paper. "Yum! Green bean casserole! My favorite!"

"Mine too," Gwen agreed. "I think Deborah's has to go in the fridge."

"Deborah said she was bringing a pistachio salad," Nicole said as she opened the refrigerator door and moved a few things around. "There, that should work." She slid Deborah's dish onto the shelf.

"Has Deborah heard from Tyler?" she asked as she straightened up.

"Last I knew, his flight was leaving on time."

"Good," Nicole said with a sigh of relief. "I know she was worried if he would even be able to get out of Denver with the storm coming."

"Uh-huh."

Nicole looked at her friend. "What?"

"Just strange, if you ask me, that he is bringing a girl to Thanksgiving dinner."

"Well, I'm happy for him. Deborah says he met her at the church he's been going to."

"That's what she said. Just seems a little quick to bring her to a family event like this. I just hope he's not rushing it."

"Tyler does not seem like the type of person to rush into

anything," Nicole said as she walked into the dining room. "I'm just happy that's he's comfortable enough to bring her here, and I can't wait to meet her."

She stopped at the dining table and double-checked the settings. Trying to get ahead of a busy day, she and Abby had set the table the night before. Nicole smiled at the beautiful oak trestle table. Marc's grandfather had made it for his bride, and now it graced her dining room. The set of china on the table had been a housewarming gift from Deborah. Deborah and Lee had gotten it for their wedding. The white china with gold rims was simple and elegant and set off the table beautifully.

"Everything looks wonderful," Gwen whispered, squeezing Nicole's arm lightly as she slid past her to go join Deborah and Abby in the living room.

"Can I get you guys anything?" Nicole asked as she leaned on the chair across from the couch where Deborah and Abby sat.

"No, we're fine," Gwen said as she motioned with her hand for Nicole to sit.

"Where's Samson?" Deborah asked. "I just realized he didn't greet us."

"He's downstairs in his crate. There was too much going on this morning. I couldn't handle him being underfoot too. I'll let him out after dinner."

"When is Tyler's flight supposed to touch down?" Gwen asked.

"Anytime," Deborah responded as she glanced at the Fitbit on her wrist.

"Did he tell you anything about this girl he's bringing?" Nicole prodded.

"Just that he met her and fell head over heels."

"Mommy, what's Uncle Tyler's friend's name?" Abby asked. She had left the sofa and was stretching up Nicole's side to get her attention.

Nicole raised an eyebrow at Deborah as she answered, "I don't really know, sweetie."

"Tyler didn't say. I guess we'll find out when he introduces her."

"Not to change the topic," Gwen said as she walked over and grabbed a deviled egg off the side buffet, "but have you heard from Reese lately?"

"Not lately," Nicole said with a shake of her head. "Last he texted, he was getting settled at his dad's place and starting to learn the business end of the company so he can start running that part. Not really much else."

"I hope he's going to continue to get help for his PTSD," Gwen said as she stuffed the deviled egg into her mouth.

"Me too," Nicole said as she glanced out the front window. A dark blue Ford Taurus had pulled into the driveway. "Looks like Tyler and his lady are here."

Deborah and Gwen stayed back in the living room as Nicole and Abby went to the front door. Tyler was just lifting his hand to knock when they swung the door open.

"Uncle Tyler!" Abby exclaimed as she jumped up and down in excitement.

Tyler chuckled as he bent over to pick Abby up. "Hi, Abby!"

An attractive young woman stood just behind him, a smile playing on her lips as she watched the exchange between the two. With heels, she appeared to be about the same height as Tyler. Her blond hair was straight and swung easily around the top edge of her shoulders. She looked up at Nicole, her ice-blue eyes showing warmth that reached her smile. She stretched her hand around Tyler and Abby and shook Nicole's.

"Hi, I'm Isabelle," she said. "It's so nice to meet you."

"It's nice to meet you too," Nicole said. "I'm Nicole, and this is my daughter, Abby."

"I feel like I know you all already," Isabelle said softly. "Tyler has talked about all of you."

Nicole raised an eyebrow to Tyler. He gave her a sideways grin as he said, "All good, I promise." Putting his free hand in the small of Isabelle's back, he guided her into the living room.

"Mom, Gwen," he began, "I want to introduce you to Isabelle Edwards." He paused a beat as a smile spread across his face before adding, "My fiancée."

Both Deborah and Gwen came to a sudden stop as they started to greet the young woman next to Tyler.

"What?" Deborah said, surprise filling her face.

"Fiancée?" Gwen added.

Nicole was the first to respond after the initial surprise. Walking over to Isabelle, she enclosed her in a warm hug and welcomed her to the family, followed by Deborah and Gwen.

"I'm sorry," Deborah stammered after she released Isabelle from her hug and held on with a hand on her arm. "Tyler gave us no idea. It's just a surprise, but a good one. Come, you two, and have a seat. We want to hear all about it."

Tyler guided Isabelle to the sofa while Gwen and Deborah each settled into matching chairs. Nicole pulled a chair from the dining table along with the tray of deviled eggs. She set the tray on the coffee table within easy reach for anyone and went into the kitchen to grab glasses of ice water with lemon wedges for everyone before sitting down finally on the chair, pulling Abby into her lap. There was an excited air and a good deal of chatter going on between the couple and Deborah and Gwen.

"Okay, get me caught up," she said as she reached for an egg. "I heard something about working together at a summer camp?"

"It was Vacation Bible School that our church runs. Tyler offered to help out with the games, and I was teaching the four- and five-year-old girls Bible story time. I can't explain it, but we connected that week." Isabelle glanced up with eyes filled with love as she added, "I hadn't really gotten to know Tyler much before that. I just saw him during the service, but after that week, things changed."

"Well, I have to admit that I noticed Isabelle right away," Tyler said as he entwined his fingers with hers and smiled down at her. "She was up front with the praise group one Sunday. She had an amazing voice, and I knew I had to meet her."

Tyler pulled his eyes from Isabelle and gave them a sheepish smile before continuing, "She is also the pastor's daughter, so I needed to tread lightly."

"Really?" Deborah said as she leaned forward. "You're a PK?"

"Yes," Isabelle said with a light laugh, "I am a pastor's kid. I have three younger siblings—twin brothers and a baby sister. I consider myself blessed in so many ways, but meeting Tyler has been the biggest blessing so far."

"Pastor Mike and I had been meeting for a few months before I started seeing Isabelle. I had a lot of questions about my faith and everything that has happened in my life since dad and Marc. He helped guide me through all the pain and pointed me back to the scriptures."

Tyler stopped and looked over to Isabelle, who smiled and squeezed his hand gently. Turning back to the others, he took a deep breath and spoke. "That's not all. I have not been happy with who I had become anymore. The constant flying around the world for work had gotten old. I have been thinking about a career change, and after talking with Pastor Mike and doing some serious praying, I've decided to go into the ministry." Tyler paused as his eyes came to meet his mother's. "I want to become a chaplain for the army, Mom. I feel like I would be honoring Dad and Marc at the same time by helping others who need it."

Nicole's eyes were moist as she looked over at Deborah to see her reaction. Deborah's hand had gone to her lips as she looked with surprise at her oldest son. With trembling hands, she reached across the coffee table that separated them and took his hand.

"Your father and brother would be so proud, as I am. You have no idea how long I have prayed that the Lord would bring you back to Him, and now you're going into ..." Sobs interrupted Deborah as she took a steadying breath. "And now you're going into ministry. This is more than I had hoped and prayed for. I am so happy."

Nicole and Gwen reached over at the same time to each put an arm on Deborah. Nicole looked over at the couple on the sofa and smiled. "What are your plans, then?"

"With my degree I already have, I can start seminary in the fall. There are a few prerequisites that I will need to take first, and I'm signed up to do most of them online. I've told my boss that I need to scale back my workload, and he's been good about it."

"Wow," Gwen said. "Are you two planning a long engagement, then?"

"Actually," Isabelle said, looking up at Tyler, "we were hoping you would like to come to Colorado for Christmas. We would like to get married on Christmas Eve."

"*What?*" Deborah exclaimed, raising her hands to her mouth. "I can't believe this, Tyler!"

"I know it's sudden," Tyler said as he leaned forward, "but we both feel like we've waited so long for this, and we want to start our life together as soon as possible. It's important to both of us that you are there for us. Will you come to our wedding, Mom?"

"Of course I will!" Deborah exclaimed. "I'm just overwhelmed. This is such good news. Just try and keep me away."

Tyler smiled with relief and then looked over at Nicole. "We would like you and Abby to come, Nicole. You're family too."

Nicole couldn't speak as emotion swirled through her. Finally, she was able to stammer out that she would be honored to come and witness their wedding. Tyler reached over and grabbed hold of her hand and squeezed it as he said, "We would also like to have Abby be our flower girl."

"Can I, Mommy?" Abby said as she pulled on Nicole's arm.

"Yes, sweetie, you can be the flower girl."

"Great!" Tyler said as he leaned back. A smile lit up both his and Isabelle's faces. "You have no idea how nervous we both were."

"Well, I can honestly say that this is going to be the best holiday we have had in a long, long time," Deborah stated firmly.

"I think I'd better check on the turkey," Nicole said, standing and wiping her eyes dry with a swipe of her hand.

"Let me help you," Gwen said, standing to join her.

"Can I help?" Isabelle offered, but Nicole waved her back into her seat.

"Gwen and I got this. There's not much left to do. You and Tyler sit back and enjoy your time with Deborah."

Gwen was already in the kitchen before Nicole got halfway across the dining room. Nicole paused at the kitchen door and looked back. Tyler had his arm around Abby as he and Isabelle both leaned forward, talking and laughing with Deborah. Peace filled Nicole's heart as she lifted her eyes to thank the one who had made it all possible.

CPSIA information can be obtained
at www.ICGtesting.com
Printed in the USA
BVHW072054020420
576762BV00001B/80

9 781973 686637